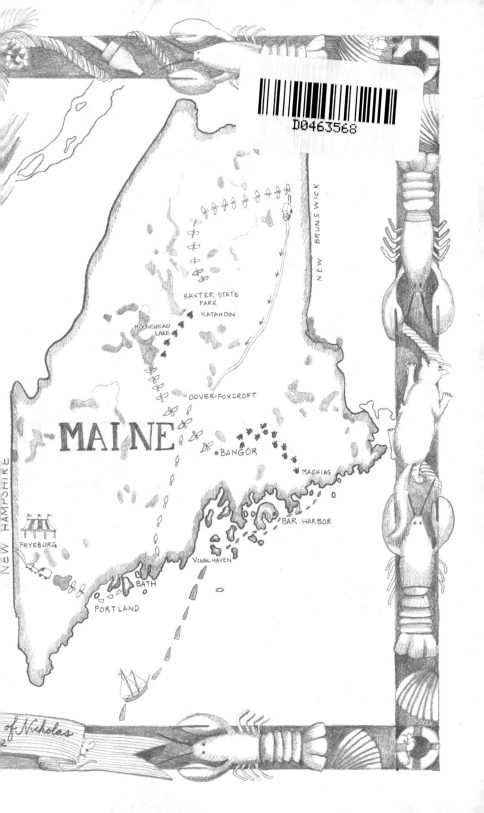

Nicholas

A MAINE TALE

by Peter Arenstam

illustrated by Karen Busch Holman

 mitten press

All inquiries should be addressed to:
Mitten Press
An imprint of Ann Arbor Media Group LLC
2500 S. State Street
Ann Arbor, MI 48104

Printed and bound by Edwards Brothers, Ann Arbor, Michigan, USA

10   9   8   7   6   5   4   3   2   1

Library of Congress Cataloging Data on File.

ISBN-13: 978-1-58726-520-4
ISBN-10: 1-58726-520-6

Book design by Somberg Design
www.sombergdesign.com

Chapter One

Nicholas, a small brown mouse, slept soundly curled up in a bed of straw in the old barn. His little paws twitched now and again as he dreamed. In the dream, his mother was making breakfast and calling out to him. A patch of sun coming through a high window moved across the floor and warmed Nicholas. He rolled over contentedly. A voice, not his mother's, reached the sleeping mouse.

"Wake up, Nicholas. You're going to miss the boat!"

Nicholas opened one eye to see an old gray-whiskered mouse leaning over him. His Uncle William, a bit on the heavy side, nudged the sleepy mouse again. "Wake up, dear boy. The boat isn't going to wait for you."

Nicholas was on the island of Martha's Vineyard in Massachusetts. He thought about his home far away in western Massachusetts. His parents were back there, rebuilding their home now after a big flood. He had come east looking for his uncle and his family journal. His cousin Francis had taken the journal to Maine, and now Nicholas had to get to Maine to continue his search. A schooner, a sailboat, sailing north would be his transportation.

The boat was leaving today, he remembered. Nicholas sat up. He looked out the window at the island farm in West Tisbury. He needed to get moving. He jumped out of bed, ran down the ladder, and toward the big door of the barn. His uncle followed along behind him.

"Now don't forget what I told you, Nicholas. The farm truck will be going into town today. You need to catch a ride to the harbor. The schooner will be leaving from the dock by noon. They have to catch the tide, so they won't wait."

Nicholas ate a hasty breakfast as he scurried out to the barnyard where the farm truck sat idling. William made a quick survey of the yard for the big gray goose. The goose liked to swim in the farm pond during the heat of the day, but sometimes he surprised them as he waddled up to the barn for his breakfast.

"I won't forget, Uncle William," Nicholas said between bites of grass seed. "Thank you for letting me stay with you for so long." Nicholas had spent the winter with his uncle, and the two mice had grown close. Although Nicholas had intended to leave as soon as spring arrived, he had lingered with his uncle well into

the summer. Ready to part at last, they hugged good-bye at the corner of the barn. Nicholas was headed for the farm truck when the old gray goose came around the corner, grumbling about his tired feet. The goose thought it was his duty to keep anyone or anything away from the property.

The goose and Nicholas saw each other at the same time. Both animals stood still for a few moments. Nicholas started to run. He headed for the truck. The goose trailed close behind. His great wings flapped up a billowing cloud of dust. Nicholas tried to stay on course for the truck. In the confusion, he headed back toward the barn. William waved from inside the barn, redirecting Nicholas. The goose beat his wings and honked, snapping his beak at the ground. Nicholas zigzagged his way around the yard.

The farmhand came out, shouted at the goose to quiet down, and then got in the truck. He rolled the truck forward, watching the goose in his mirror. Nicholas heard the truck, dashed toward it, and jumped onto the tailgate. The truck bounced out of the yard and down the lane. The old goose stamped his foot and honked again, satisfied that he had done his duty. Nicholas, holding onto the truck with one paw, waved to his uncle.

William, watching from the barn door, waved after Nicholas. He silently wished the young mouse luck. He knew Nicholas had been through a lot in the past year. Now, William thought, Nicholas is headed Down East to Maine. It was a much bigger state and he hoped he had prepared Nicholas for everything to come.

William returned to his rooms. He had promised he would return to the Berkshires to help Nicholas's parents rebuild their home after the terrible flood. "There is so much to do," William said aloud to himself, looking around his rooms. "I'm getting too old for all this adventure," he added, rubbing his back.

Chapter Two

Young Nicholas had made many trips to the waterfront during his stay with his Uncle William. Nicholas knew to look for the long white schooner tied to the dock near a sign with a painted black dog. The crew had been putting supplies aboard for the final leg of its voyage. Uncle William had pointed out the boat to Nicholas and had told him the schooner was the best way for Nicholas to reach Maine.

When Nicholas arrived at the waterfront, he didn't see the schooner at the dock. He ran back and forth along the shore in hopes of finding the boat. Nicholas spotted a wharf rat nosing into a dumpster near a boat-building shed. "Excuse me, sir. What happened to the long white schooner that was tied up to this dock?" Nicholas said, trying his best to sound brave.

The wharf rat squinted at the small mouse while he sucked on an old chicken bone. "You looking to ship out, young fella?" The rat gnawed on the chicken bone briefly. "That schooner left fifteen minutes ago. You just missed her. She's out in the channel by now, I suspect. I can get you aboard an oil tanker headed for the Far East if you're lookin' to ship out."

"No, thank you. I'm on my way to Maine and I was supposed to get aboard that schooner," Nicholas replied.

"Maine, you say. Why didn't you speak up? I got my sea legs aboard the old *Scotia Prince* out of Portland, Maine. Bound for Nova Scotia, we were, over the meanest patch of water on the Atlantic seaboard," the rat rambled on.

"I really need to get aboard that schooner. I must find my cousin, who lives in Maine," Nicholas interrupted. He could see the boat making its way down the channel.

"Right you are, my young shipmate. Let me take you in tow. I'll get you alongside the schooner before she clears the breakwater."

The rat jumped down from the dumpster and ran with Nicholas under the pier. "Climb aboard," the rat said, gesturing to part of an old plank resting on the sand near the water. Nicholas scrambled up and held on with all four paws. The rat shoved the plank into the water and paddled along with his back paws. "I've used this trick many times," the rat said, as he floated the plank out into the harbor.

In no time, a passing motorboat sped by, with lines and fenders trailing in the water. "Hold on tight," the rat said. He grabbed the trailing line, and the plank skipped along behind the boat, bouncing over the waves.

"Summer people," the rat said over his shoulder to Nicholas, "can always be counted on to trail lines in the water." The motorboat, full with a family, a beach umbrella, toys, and the family dog, headed out of the harbor for a day at a nearby beach. When the boat approached the schooner, the rat swung in close, still holding onto the towline.

"Reach for the anchor line," the rat said to Nicholas. The schooner's anchor dangled from the cathead and a loop of anchor line trailed in the water. Nicholas leapt. He scrambled up the line to the deck of the schooner. Looking back, he saw that the rat still held tightly to the motorboat's towline. He sped away, waving to Nicholas. "Fair winds and a safe voyage, my young friend. I'm off for a bit of shore leave myself."

"Thank you," Nicholas shouted after the rat. "You've been very kind. Good-bye!"

Nicholas turned away from his new friend and looked over the deck of the schooner. The long wooden deck swept back away from the bow. The plank seams reminded Nicholas of newly plowed furrows in a field. The crew worked, raising the large canvas sails, coiling lines, and stowing gear. All the way in the stern, the captain stood behind a spoked wheel, steering the schooner out to sea.

Nicholas, hungry after all the excitement of the morning, sniffed about for something to eat. He made his way along the side of the cabin house and found an open porthole. His whiskers twitching, he climbed in and landed with a thud in the galley. A cook, busy building a fire in the old-fashioned stove, didn't notice the tiny brown mouse. An overhead cupboard door swung open and closed again with the rolling of the schooner. A parakeet, sitting in a swinging cage, watched Nicholas search for a place to hide.

"Don't let the cook see you. Don't let the cook see you," the caged bird warned. "Climb up and hide in the cupboard. Hide in the cupboard," the bird added. To the cook it sounded like the parakeet was chirping and singing a nonsense song. Nicholas, who understood the bird, made his way up the side of the cabin and jumped into the open cupboard door.

Nicholas was safe on board and secure in the cupboard. He sat in the dark alone. He moved some cans labeled B&M Baked Beans to make a space in the back of the cupboard for a bed. He lay down, happy to be on his way to Maine at last. He nibbled on a few crackers he found in the cupboard and then let the rolling ship rock him to sleep.

Chapter Three

It was dark when Nicholas awoke. He smelled wood smoke from the stove. Nicholas peeked out the cupboard door. A kerosene lantern, turned down low, dimly lit the cabin. The parakeet's cage swung nearby. The bird sat on a perch with her eyes closed. "Psst," Nicholas whispered. "Psst. Miss Parakeet, are you awake?"

The parakeet ruffled her feathers but kept her eyes closed. "Land ho, land ho," she chirped in her sleep. "All hands take in the sail."

"Miss Parakeet, wake up, please," Nicholas said. The bird opened her eyes.

"Hello there. I'm Pattie, Pretty Pattie. You must be the stowaway, the stowaway, who came aboard in Massachusetts," the parakeet said.

"I'm Nicholas. Is this schooner headed for Maine?"

"We'll be in Penobscot Bay by noon tomorrow, by noon tomorrow," the bird sang. "Where are you bound?"

"I'm headed to Maine to find someone from my family," Nicholas said. "He's a cousin named Francis. It's very important that I find him."

"Maine's a big state, young Nicholas, a big state. I hope you know where to look."

"All I know is Francis lives in Maine and he has a family journal that I need to get back." Just then, a little white dog with brown spots skittered into the cabin.

"Arf, arf, arf, who are you talking to, Pattie?" the Jack Russell terrier said. The dog bounced up and down, trying to reach the cage. "Who is it? Who is it? Do I know him?" the dog yipped.

"Calm down, Scupper. No, you don't know him," Pattie said. "Scupper, here," she said to Nicholas, "is just a puppy. They named him for a deck drain because he is always falling down and nearly being washed overboard. The captain makes him wear a life jacket all the time on the schooner."

"Hello, Scupper," Nicholas said. Scupper spun in circles showing off his doggy life jacket. After a few minutes, he landed with a plop on the deck and looked up at Nicholas.

"It's almost time to wake the cook. I'm hungry. What do you eat? The cook feeds me three times a day because I'm a growing puppy. Are you all grown up? The cook says he has half a mind to leave me ashore next time, but he never does. Are you going ashore?" Scupper bounded onto a bench, then back to the deck. He sniffed in a corner, then barked at a shadow.

"I'm going ashore when we get to Maine," Nicholas said, trying to follow the dog around the cabin with his eyes.

"We're all going ashore at Vinalhaven. I heard the captain tell the cook," Scupper said to Nicholas. "I'm to go with them. The captain said I can run around all I want on shore."

On deck, a bell softly rang out. "It's the change of the watch, change of the watch. New crew on deck, Scupper," Pattie said. "Take Nicholas up on deck. The sun is coming up. We should be getting close to the islands by now. He might like to see Maine."

"Climb on, Nicholas. I am the best at getting up on deck. You can hide in the collar of my life jacket."

Nicholas hunkered down inside the life jacket and held on tightly as Scupper sprung up the stairs to the deck. Everything was wet with mist.

"I can run from the bow to the stern in five seconds flat. Do you want to see me do it?" Scupper said as he started to run forward.

Nicholas held on tightly. Scupper skidded this way and that as the boat rolled in the waves. Suddenly, Scupper, stumbling over a line stretched across the boat, slid and tumbled into the water.

"Watch out," Nicholas yelled out too late. He jumped from the life jacket, landing on the rail as Scupper splashed in the water. The dog paddled madly alongside the slow-moving schooner. Nicholas looked back at the helmsman. He was speaking to his replacement. Nicholas ran to the ship's bell. He leapt at the lanyard, ringing the bell fiercely. The crew looked up to see little Scupper splashing in the water next to the boat. They acted quickly, throwing a life ring on a line into the water.

Scupper held onto the ring as the crew dragged him back aboard. Scupper barked happily, shook briskly, and sniffed up and down the deck looking for Nicholas. He found the mouse hiding in a coil of line hung on a pin rail.

"Did you see me swimming? I am the best swimmer on the boat. The cook says that sometimes he'd like to see me swim home. I bet I could do it. Did you see me, Nicholas?"

"Yes, I saw the whole thing, Scupper. I think you need to be more careful on a boat. You can get in real trouble. Edward and I learned that on a fishing boat out of Gloucester. Edward is a chipmunk friend of mine. We traveled all over the state of Massachusetts together. I miss him. He didn't like being out on the water very much. Once, we helped keep the fishing boat from sinking."

As the two animals talked, streaks of fog flowed in around the boat. Warm air, flowing up from the south, hit the cold waters of Maine and made fog. The schooner was sailing alone on the sea. The sun was gone. The horizon was gone. They rolled on, as if sailing in a cloud in the sky.

In a hushed voice, for once, Scupper spoke to Nicholas. "We are off the coast of Maine now. We won't see anything until we are very close to the islands."

Nicholas looked up. The mist swirled around the moving boat. He shivered and worried about finding his cousin when he couldn't see anything ahead. He missed his family and he missed his friend Edward.

Chapter Four

The schooner sailed on through the morning. Scupper had gone below to see if the cook needed help making lunch. The fog had thinned out, but had not gone away completely. Someone chimed eight bells, which meant it was noon. Nicholas looked up to see dark green shapes looming ahead.

As the schooner approached, the green shapes turned into trees growing along a rocky shoreline.

Nicholas saw seagulls flapping slowly through the sky, terns hovering over the water looking for lunch, and sea ducks swimming out of the path of the boat.

Nicholas sniffed the air. The scent of sea salt mixed with the smell of earth and the sharp tang of spruce trees. A green bell buoy ahead beckoned them to the harbor. The crew came on deck, lowered the sails, and started the engine. Nicholas hopped from the coil. He peeked through the bow rail while the skipper steered the boat to a dock.

At the dock, lobstermen unloaded traps, a truck on the pier delivered ice, and fishermen wearing black rubber boots and orange rain pants went about their business. Summer visitors watched everything from behind the railing of the pier. Ice cream cones dripped over their hands in the hot sun. Nicholas noticed a young seagull sitting on a piling.

"Excuse me," Nicholas asked, scrambling down the dock line to the pier, "where am I?"

The seagull stood up, stretched his neck forward, flapped his wings, and called out, "Kyow, kyow, kyow." Nicholas looked up at the seabird, puzzled. The bird lifted off the piling and slowly flew out over the harbor.

Scupper came bouncing along the dock toward Nicholas. "Welcome to Maine, Nicholas. Don't mind that old bird," Scupper said. "Sea gulls like to keep to themselves. They make a lot of noise, but they don't mean any harm. Come with me. I'm going for a run onshore."

Nicholas scrambled up Scupper's life jacket again. The dog bolted away from the pier, heading into the small town. From the schooner, Nicholas heard the cook calling for the dog, but Scupper paid no attention.

"Slow down, Scupper. I can't hold on when you bounce around like this," Nicholas said. He slid from one side of the life jacket to the other as the dog sniffed interesting smells here and there. "Where are we, Scupper?

"This is Vinalhaven, of course," Scupper said. "We stop here all the time. I want to show you around. There is the best swimming hole just outside of town. Do you want to go swimming? I am the best swimmer."

Nicholas didn't get a chance to answer. Scupper yipped at a butterfly. Then he yapped at a honeybee looking for flowers. He followed the winding road up a hill, around a corner, and past the last house of the little fishing village. The trees grew thick in places. Nicholas could still hear the ding of the bell buoy out in the harbor.

Scupper bounded forward to a clearing, yipping excitedly. Through the trees, Nicholas saw a pool of water. On three sides of the pool, the edges were steep granite. On one side, large steps, cut as if for a giant, descended into the water. Scupper barked and sniffed at a small painted mound in the dirt. To Nicholas's surprise, a head and four legs popped out of the mound. The turtle looked up at Scupper.

"Now there, Scupper. You gave me a fright, I should

say. You just sit down now and tell me what you've been up to since I saw you last."

"How've you been, Burt? This is my new friend Nicholas. We're going swimming. Do you want to go swimming? How's the water?"

"How do you do, sir?" Nicholas said. "I've never seen a pond look like this. What are the giant steps for?"

"This isn't a pond at all. This is an old quarry. Men mined granite from this island for years. There is Maine granite in statues, bridges, and monuments all over the country," Burt said. "In time, the old quarries filled up with water. This quarry is now used as a town swimming hole." The slow-moving turtle said all this as he made his way toward the water. Nicholas walked along with him. Scupper raced back and forth, from the edge of the quarry to the turtle.

"Who wants to go in? I'm diving right in." Scupper wagged his short tail and barked at the water. He looked out over the edge. It looked like a long way to the water. The hard, gray granite plunged into the clear water. Scupper could see the rock continue deep down below the surface.

"Hey, I know what! Instead of swimming, let's head back into town. I bet the cook is looking for me. We really should get back. Come on."

"He does this every time he comes to the quarry," Burt said to Nicholas.

Scupper trotted down the road, turned around, and came back. "Come on, Nicholas, you don't want me to leave you here, do you? Hop on."

"Good-bye, Burt," Nicholas waved, and thought to himself, "I never even got to ask Burt about my cousin. It is tiring keeping up with this wiry little dog."

Chapter Five

The pair made their way back to town. Nicholas did his best to hold onto Scupper. At the top of a hill overlooking the town, they stopped at a park. In the middle of the park, a huge four-wheeled cart stood under an open shed. Nicholas hopped down. Scupper barked at two pigeons cooing to each other under the roof of the shed.

Nicholas scrambled up the huge back wheel of the cart. He could see out to the harbor from the top of the eight-foot-high wheel.

"Well, hello there," Nicholas said to the pair of granite-colored pigeons. The birds continued their own conversation.

"Excuse me. Lovely day, isn't it?" Nicholas said. "My friend and I are from that boat tied to the dock in town."

"It's a fairly good day. I suspect the fog will be back when the tide starts to flood," one pigeon said.

"Oh, I don't know about that," the other pigeon said. "The winds turned around now. We're due for a dry spell, I should say."

"Dry spell? That mackerel sky says otherwise," the first pigeon said. "We'll see rain before tomorrow."

"My dad always said, 'If you don't like the weather in New England, just wait a minute,'" Nicholas said, trying to get into the conversation.

Scupper tugged at a block of wood at the bottom of one wheel. He growled and gripped the wood in his little teeth. The cart gave a lurch.

"Be careful, Scupper," Nicholas said. "This cart is starting to shake."

"That cart," the first pigeon said, "is called a galamander."

"It's about one hundred years old," the second pigeon added. "The quarry men used it to move huge blocks of granite to the carver's yard. They cut the stone into statues. We're partial to the history of statues, you know," the pigeon added.

Scupper wasn't paying any attention. He had gotten it into his head that he wanted to remove the block from the wheel. He tugged and tugged until the block flew out. He landed with a thud and rolled down the hill toward town. The cart creaked loudly.

"Scupper, no!" Nicholas shouted. It was too late. The cart started rolling slowly out of the shed. It picked up speed as it lumbered backward down the hill away from town.

The two pigeons took flight, Nicholas shouted, and Scupper picked up his ears. The cook was calling from the boat. Scupper thought this was a good time to head back to the schooner, and he bounded away toward the

harbor. Nicholas still clung to the fast-moving galamander as it bounced over the road at the bottom of
the hill. He lost his grip, flew into the air, and landed in
a beach rose bush.

Nicholas lay in the bush stunned. The light was pink,
filtered through the rose petals. He felt the bush's
thorny stem sticking into his side. The pigeons landed
on the ground next to the bush.

"Well, I didn't expect that to happen," one pigeon
said.

"No, can't say I did, either," the other pigeon said. "It
reminds me of the time my dad used to tell of Liberty,
the old farmer's mare. Seems she ran off down the road
still hooked to a plow. Thinking quickly, the farmer ran
after her, planting potatoes in the furrow."

"That's what you've got to do," the first pigeon said.
"You've got to make the best of a bad situation."

Nicholas crawled out of the bush, his head still dizzy
from the wild ride. The two pigeons had already started
on another story. Nicholas wandered off, thinking he
should try to get back up to the top of the hill. When he
finally made it, he couldn't believe what he saw.

The schooner, with Scupper standing on the rail in the stern, was making its way out of the harbor. Nicholas watched as crew members raised the sails. The boat moved around a point of land and sailed out of sight.

Nicholas sat on the grass on the hilltop. He was alone on this island. He thought his friend Edward would have known what to do. Thinking of his old friend made him sad. Nicholas wandered down the hill, searching for a place to spend the night. He stumbled over the rocky shore. It was quiet except for the sound of the wind in the trees and the waves washing over the rocks.

Nicholas found a spruce tree near the shore tipped at an odd angle. The roots, pulled out of the ground by some storm, made a kind of cave. He crawled under the tree. The ground was pebbly and dry. Wild berries grew nearby, and he was safe. Nicholas gathered some moss and pine needles for a bed. He curled up in his new home and wondered how he would ever get off the island to find his cousin.

Chapter Six

Nicholas spent time on Vinalhaven. He traveled through the forests, watched the lobstermen haul traps near shore, and listened to passing boats toot at each other in the ever-present fog. One day he noticed a small sailboat anchored near the shore. A man, woman, and a young boy got into a dinghy and rowed toward the island.

The family came ashore near Nicholas's cave. The little boy wore big black rubber boots. As soon as he got out of the dinghy, he ran along the shore swinging a green plastic bucket in one hand. The parents walked slowly, letting the little boy wander. He looked in tide pools and under rocks as he walked. He filled his bucket with treasures.

He wandered over to the spruce tree tipped to one side. He peered into the small cave. Inside, Nicholas looked out at the small boy. He scrambled to the back of the cave.

The boy reached his hand in and called to Nicholas. "Come here, little fella," he said. "I won't hurt you."

Nicholas sniffed the air, twitched his whiskers, and held on to the end of his tail.

The boy said, "That's all right. Are you hungry?" The boy reached into his pocket and pulled out a small package of crackers. He offered one to Nicholas. "Here you go. I bet you're hungry."

Nicholas was hungry. He was lonely and this little boy seemed friendly. Nicholas nibbled at the cracker.

The little boy squatted down and watched him eat. "There you go, my friend. Are you all alone?" The boy reached out and stroked Nicholas on the back. "Do you want to come with me on my boat?"

Nicholas looked at the boy.

"My parents and I are sailing along the whole coast of Maine this summer. I could use a friend, too." The boy smiled and picked up Nicholas. "I'll put you in the pocket of my parka. Stay in there until we get on the boat." The boy flipped the pocket closed and walked over to his parents who were waiting by the dinghy.

"Come on, Timmy," the boy's mother said. "It's time to go."

Timmy didn't want to tell them about the mouse in his rain parka pocket.

The sailboat was much smaller than the schooner. The little boy had his own bunk in the forward cabin. He had decorated the bunk with driftwood, shells, and bits of old lobster buoys he found along the shore. "I'll make a bed for you," the boy said. He used an empty tissue box and put some more crackers inside. "There you go," he said, setting Nicholas down in the box.

Nicholas sailed with Timmy and his parents, visiting many islands and long peninsulas off the Maine coast. Nicholas thought he might find his cousin living on one of the islands. They sailed from Casco Bay to Machais Bay. Some islands, like Mount Desert, were busy with tourists, lobstermen, and summer residents. The islands Nicholas liked best were the ones where no one lived. On every island where they stopped, Nicholas asked about his cousin Francis.

Timmy talked to Nicholas all the time. Nicholas listened and learned about seals and dolphins in the sea. He learned about osprey and terns in the air. He learned about one bird that could fly in the sky and in the water. Timmy said the bird made him laugh when he looked at it, but they could be tough when they were protecting their homes.

One day Timmy and his family went ashore on an island called Eastern Egg Rock. Timmy set Nicholas down among the lichen-covered rocks and told him not to wander far. Timmy set to catching small fish in his green bucket.

Nicholas could hear a deep whirring sound coming from underground. He crept along carefully. He peered into dark little burrows and around rounded boulders. He did not see what was making such a strange sound.

All at once, a black-and-white bird popped out of the ground. She had a colorful beak and waddled on her webbed feet. She moved liked she was on a mission.

"My chick is hungry. It wants more krill. All day I fish for it. Now, let me by," the bird said.

Nicholas jumped back out of the way and followed the bird down the path.

"Do you live here, ma'am?" Nicholas asked. "Have you seen a mouse like me around here, ma'am? His name is Francis."

"Don't call me ma'am. My name is Mildred. There are no mice here. This is a puffin colony. I don't care for mice myself." The puffin shook and groomed her feathers with her orange bill. "My chick is waiting for fish." The puffin huffed along, ready to wade into the water. "Don't call me ma'am," she mumbled.

"Wait! Don't go Mildred," Nicholas said. "I want to talk to you. My friend Timmy has buckets of fish. He will share them with you."

"Buckets of fish, you say," the puffin said and stopped in her tracks. "Where is this Timmy?"

Nicholas shrugged. "I'm looking for my cousin Francis. Can you help me find him?"

Mildred tilted her head sideways and stared at Nicholas with her glassy eye. "You lead me to this bucket of fish and I'll help you."

Nicholas said, "Follow me. We have to move quietly so we don't scare Timmy."

"Move quietly? Are you saying I can't move quietly?" Mildred squawked, flapped her wings, and shook her head.

They made their way to the cove where the green bucket stood alone, full of seawater and tiny fish. Timmy was examining a sea urchin he had found in a tide pool.

"Go on, help yourself," Nicholas urged.

Mildred stuck her head in the bucket. She came up, dripping water, and holding five small fish, all arranged head-to-tail in her beak.

Timmy looked up. "Hey you, come back here with my fish," he shouted.

The startled bird took flight. She headed back to her burrow and her hungry young chick. Nicholas sat down on the cold stones. He held his head in his paws.

"How am I ever going to find my cousin?" he thought. It seemed hopeless. So far, all he had seen were islands, water, and more islands.

Mildred landed again next to Nicholas. "A deal is a deal," she said as she scooped Nicholas up by the tail with her beak and flew off. "Now don't squirm around, or I'll drop you in the sea," Mildred mumbled.

Nicholas closed his eyes and tried to imagine where this bird might be taking him.

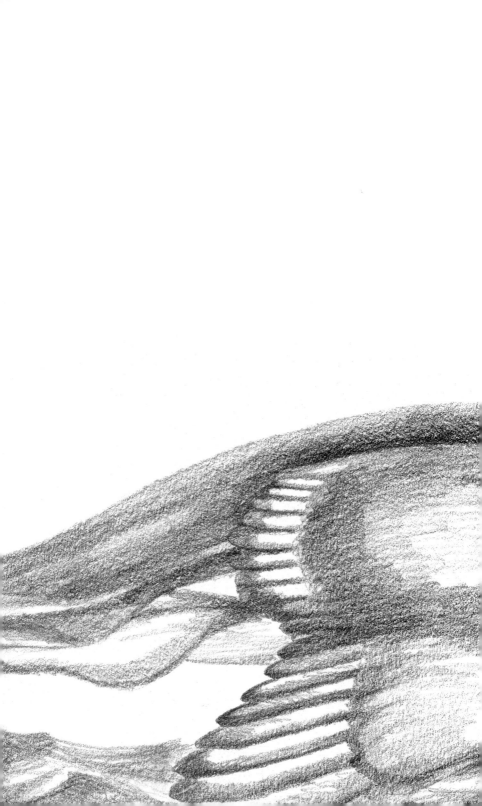

Chapter Seven

Mildred flew through the night, skimming over wave tops. Nicholas, dangling from her orange beak by his tail, splashed along. He sputtered and coughed. He did not like it. The salt water was cold. He was tired, sad, and his tail hurt. He tried his best to sleep.

Nicholas stirred as Mildred landed in the water. They surfed through the waves to a rocky shoreline. In an unusual show of grace, she delicately put Nicholas down on a tuft of grass.

"Oh, my beak is killing me," the puffin said. "I thought I was going to drop you once or twice. But, I did enjoy stretching my wings a bit. It is a nice break from feeding the young one."

"Thank you for the ride," Nicholas said. "I hope you are going to be all right."

"I'll be fine. I might spend a day or two up here and let my mate take care of the chick. I have relations of my own out on Machias Seal Island. There are more puffins on that island than you can shake a sand lance at. There's a lot of gossip to catch up on."

Nicholas looked around. "Where am I?" There was not much to see. Low bushes and tall grass grew in the rising landscape. Granite boulders dotted the fields. Stands of spruce, cedar, and hackmatack trees stood off in the distance.

"You are in the best place to find your cousin I can think of," Mildred said. "These are the blueberry barrens. Mice families come here to eat the little berries and live among the tall trees."

"Do you think my cousin lives up here?" Nicholas asked.

"You won't know until you look. I have to go now. I can't wait to tell the other puffins about carrying a mouse all the way up here. They won't believe it." Mildred dove back in the water, paddled her webbed feet, and took off into the air.

Nicholas headed inland toward the stand of trees. The unripe blueberries were still small, white, and oval-shaped. Nicholas tried some, but found them bitter and waxy. He nibbled on some spruce seeds and wondered what he should do next.

He looked out over the barrens. The granite boul-

ders made all sorts of shapes. This one looked like a paper wasp's nest. The one on a rise near the trees looked like a small black bear. That cluster of rocks looked like a clutch of rabbits discussing the news. Nicholas paused. He looked back at the rock shaped like a bear. "Hadn't it been closer to the trees before?" he thought.

Nicholas watched closely. The rock appeared to be moving slowly toward him. With growing alarm, Nicholas realized that it was a real live black bear! He squeaked and took off up a tree. The bear snuffed and snorted as it ate its way through the unripe berries.

The bear stopped. He spotted the mouse and shuffled over to the trees. He stood on his hind legs and put his front paws on the tree trunk above Nicholas.

"Hey, watcha' doin' little mouse?" the bear asked. "Do you live around here?"

"Don't eat me," Nicholas managed to say with his eyes shut.

"Eat you? I don't want to eat you. I'm full of berries. I couldn't eat you now if I wanted to, which I don't."

"I just arrived here," Nicholas said. "I'm looking for my cousin Francis. He's a mouse like me. He lives in Maine. Mildred, a puffin who brought me here, said I might find him here."

"There were a lot of mice. I mean, earlier in the spring many mice lived around here," the bear cub said. "To tell you the truth, when we bears came out of hibernation, most of the mice left," he shrugged.

"I'm getting tired of holding onto this tree. Do you think I can get down?" Nicholas asked.

"Sure, let's go sit out in the sun. I'm Nathan."

"I'm Nicholas. Where's your family?"

"I'm old enough to be on my own," Nathan said proudly. "My mom has my new little sister to look out for this year. I can fend for myself." Nathan stood on his hind legs when he said this.

"I miss my family," Nicholas said.

"I kind of miss my mom, too," Nathan said. "She's so busy with my little sister that she doesn't have time for me." Nathan sighed and looked sad.

"Why don't you come with me?" Nicholas asked. "You can help me find my cousin, and we can keep each other company."

"I bet I know where all the mice went. When it warms up, the mice like to stay in the shade of the trees.

There's a big forest near here. All kinds of animals live in the forest. We can ask if anyone has seen your cousin."

"I don't know," Nicholas said. "It sounds like there might be too many trees for us to find some little mice in such a big forest."

"I'll show you how to cover some ground," Nathan said. "I may be a big bear, but I can move when I want to. Hop on." Nicholas clung to the fur on the back of Nathan's neck as Nathan loped into the trees.

Chapter Eight

Nicholas and Nathan followed the Machias River away from the coast and into the forests of spruce, pine, maple, and oak trees. They talked as Nathan shuffled along. He told Nicholas about his home in the north woods. Nicholas talked about his adventures since he left his home. Nicholas liked to travel in the dappled sunlight among the trees. They stopped often to listen to the quiet sounds of the forest.

A chickadee hopped along a tree branch overhead. They could hear the river in the distance tumbling along its course.

"It is so peaceful here," Nicholas said. "It feels like nothing has changed here for years and years."

"My mom told me that lumbermen worked in this forest at one time," Nathan said. "They lived in camps in the woods all winter. Every day they went out with big handsaws and axes to fell trees. In the springtime, they sent the logs down the river to sawmills on the coast."

"Some of the old camps are still out here in the forest," Nathan said. "People use them for hunting and fishing. Maybe your mouse cousin lives in one of the cabins."

"Do you think so?" Nicholas asked. "That would be great. I haven't seen my own family for a long time. It would nice to find the journal and go home."

"There is a cabin over by a big bend in the river. Let's go take a look."

The two animals stepped carefully out of the trees near the river. Ahead, an old log cabin stood in a clearing. Small ash, red oaks, and hemlock trees grew in thickets around the cabin.

Nicholas saw an old man wearing a red-and-black-checkered shirt and dirty brown pants near the cabin door. He was chopping firewood. He had a pile of split wood surrounding his feet. His sweat-stained green cap stood tilted back on his head. "That ought to do for now," the old man said, looking at the pile. "Warm work," he added, wiping his brow with a red handkerchief.

Nicholas scurried out of his hiding spot and ran toward the cabin. Nathan, too late to stop Nicholas, set out after him. "Wait, Nicholas, that old man might not like mice," Nathan said, trying to catch Nicholas.

The old man had his back to the animals as he gathered firewood. When the old man turned around, Nicholas scurried between his legs and through the door. Nathan skidded to a stop right in front of the frightened man.

Nathan snuffed at the man. The man stared at Nathan. The old man shouted, threw the wood into the air, and ran for the kitchen door. In the top of a tall pine, a blue jay squawked about all the noise. Nathan sat down with a humph, alone outside, and wondered what would become of Nicholas.

Nicholas, inside the cabin now, scurried along near the kitchen wall. The man, looking out the window at Nathan, didn't notice. Nicholas came to a small pantry and squeezed under the door. Inside, boxes and barrels of supplies lined the room.

"Hello," Nicholas called out, "is anybody in here?" If there were mice about, Nicholas knew they would certainly be near this pantry.

From inside a wooden box Nicholas heard a faint "Who's out there? Go away, and leave us alone."

"I just want to talk with you. Don't be afraid of me," Nicholas said.

There was a lot of squeaking and scurrying inside the box. Nicholas saw a little nose and whiskers peek out. "Is there anyone out there with you?" the mouse asked.

"I'm alone now," Nicholas said. "But I came here with my friend Nathan."

"You're alone?" the mouse said, sticking his head out of the box. "Who's Nathan?"

"He's a young bear I am traveling with—" Nicholas started.

"A bear!" the mouse shrieked, and disappeared back into the box.

"It's all right," Nicholas called into the box. "He's my friend. He wouldn't hurt you. I'm looking for my cousin. Do you know him? His name is Francis and he lives in Maine."

The scared mouse crept out of the box. "Maine's a big state, you know. We came from Bangor. We're city mice. We want to get out of this cabin and out of these woods."

"Who is in there with you?" Nicholas asked. "And, how did you end up out here in this cabin?"

"My wife and I. We're expecting little ones soon. We made a nest in the box while it was still in the warehouse in Bangor. They delivered the box to this cabin. We tried to find our way back to the city, but there are a lot of wild animals and wild noises in this forest. We've been hiding in the box for a week."

"Are there a lot of mice where you live in Bangor? Maybe Francis lives in a city," Nicholas said. "If I help you get home, will you help me look for my cousin in Bangor?"

"We'd do anything to get back to the city," the scared mouse said.

"You wait here. I will go talk with my friend Nathan. Maybe he can help us."

Nicholas left the mouse pair huddled together in their box and went back to the kitchen. The old man was still there. He was sitting at his table, loading an ancient shotgun.

Nicholas knew he had to go outside, warn his friend Nathan, and talk to him about helping the two lost mice. First, Nicholas needed a plan.

Chapter Nine

The old man with the red-and-black-checkered shirt stood at the small square window next to the kitchen door. He held an ancient, rusted shotgun in his hand.

"Where's that bear at?" the man muttered to himself. "I won't tolerate black bears getting into my cabin."

As Nicholas sat trying to figure out what to do, he heard a rap-tap-tap on the front door.

"Who's that?" the man said.

Rap-tap-tap went the sound again. The man took one more look out the back window and went to the front door. When he opened the door, a downy wood-pecker flew in.

"You get now!" the man said. Dropping the shotgun,

he chased the bird through the cabin, leaving the front door open. A porcupine waddled up the steps and into the cabin.

"Where did you come from?" the man asked. The man backed into the kitchen away from the porcupine. The woodpecker followed. Grabbing a broom, the man tried to swat at the bird. He kept an eye on the porcupine.

The man led the woodpecker to the open door as a white-striped skunk pointed his nose into the cabin. The man retreated to the kitchen again. The woodpecker swooped back into the house. The skunk nodded at the porcupine and both animals went after the man. He stood on a chair in the kitchen, swinging his broom harmlessly at the animals.

Nicholas saw what was happening. "We have a chance to get out of this cabin," Nicholas said to the two mice. "Close your eyes and hold onto my tail." The mice were anxious to get out, so they did as Nicholas asked.

The porcupine said to Nicholas, "Nathan told us you needed some help. He's waiting for you at the river."

"We'll keep the man busy until you get away," the skunk added.

"Thank you," Nicholas said over his shoulder. He hurried out of the cabin with the two mice in tow. "Good luck finding your cousin," the woodpecker said as he flew through the room.

Nathan sat by the river licking his paws and smacking his lips. "Have you ever had rainbow trout?" he asked Nicholas. "It is quite delicious. I highly recommend it."

The two mice, who had kept their eyes closed the entire time, opened them and looked up at the bear. "Ah," they shouted, "a bear!" They took off back toward the cabin.

"I get that all the time," Nathan said to Nicholas. "They'll be back. They won't like all the animals in the cabin."

The two mice stopped near the cabin door. They looked in and then back at Nicholas and Nathan.

"He's all right," Nicholas said. "He's my friend, and you two are my friends, so we can travel together."

The mice crept closer to the bear. He smiled at them, showing his big white teeth. "Are you sure?" they asked.

Nicholas climbed up on the bear's neck. Nathan giggled like a young boy.

"Nicholas, that tickles." Nathan squirmed around.

The old man ran out of the cabin followed by the woodpecker, the porcupine, and the skunk.

Nathan held out his paw. "Let's go while we have a chance," he said. The mice stepped onto the pads of his paw, and he raised them up and deposited them next to Nicholas.

"Hold on," Nicholas said. Nathan loped away using his fastest bear gait.

"Those animals will leave the old man alone as soon

as we're gone," Nathan said. He lumbered along until the cabin and the other animals were out of sight. It was quiet again except for the sound of the river and the wind in the trees.

"Thank you for helping us out of that cabin, Nathan," Nicholas said. Nathan had slowed to a walk. They came out of the trees along a dirt road. "I don't think I could have done it on my own."

"So who are these two mice we have with us?" Nathan asked.

"My name is Seth and this is Sarah." The two mice clung tightly to Nathan's fur, but nodded.

"They will never believe it back in Bangor when we tell them we rode on top of a bear," Sarah said.

"Bangor?" Nathan asked. "Are you two headed for Bangor?"

"That's right," Seth said. "And Nicholas here is coming with us. We might be able to help him find his cousin."

"Are you going to Bangor, too, Nicholas?" Nathan asked. He stopped by a pile of logs stacked in a clearing.

"Do you want to come with us, Nathan? I'm sure we could have some fun in the city," Nicholas said.

"Bears and cities don't mix," Nathan said. "People kind of get excited when they see a bear coming down the road."

"How far is Bangor from here?" Nicholas asked.

"It is a very long walk," Nathan said. "I can get you

a ride, though. Big trucks headed downstate stop here to pick up logs. They all go through Bangor."

Nicholas, Seth, and Sarah hopped down from Nathan and crawled up into the log pile.

"Just stay out of sight among the logs. Soon enough a lumber truck will be here to pick up this load," Nathan said. "Good-bye, Nicholas. I hope you find your cousin. You are a good friend for spending some time with me."

"Good-bye, Nathan. Where will you go now?"

"I think I'll go look for Mom and my little sister." With that, Nathan wandered back into the forest. Long shadows stretched across the dirt road. Brown bats appeared overhead in the twilight, scooping up insects. Nicholas and the two city mice sat on the pile of logs in the gathering dark wondering how long they would have to wait for their ride to Bangor.

Chapter Ten

The deep rumble of a diesel engine and a flash of bright lights woke the mice. It was early morning. From where Nicholas lay tucked among the pile of pine logs, he could see the stars giving way to blue sky. An empty logging truck idled next to the logs.

A man climbed down from the cab and went around to the back of the truck. He used a set of claws attached to the end of a boom to grab logs, two or three at a time. He loaded them onto his truck. Nicholas and his new friends were on the last logs to be loaded. They ended up on the top of the pile on the truck.

With the logs secured, the driver started the truck and rolled down the dirt road. Soon the truck was speeding along the winding road, leaning into the curves and lifting over the hills.

The two city mice crouched down among the logs. Seth and Sarah kept their backs to the wind and held each other. Nicholas enjoyed the view of the passing trees. He waved to a woodchuck browsing in the grass by the side of the road. The woodchuck munched a stalk of grass, unconcerned with the fast-moving truck.

Nicholas crawled down to Seth and Sarah. "Wow, this is almost like flying," Nicholas said. "You should come up and take a look around."

"We'll look around when we stop," Seth said. "I don't think this is very safe."

"I can see buildings ahead," Nicholas said. "We must be near the city."

There were more cars on the road as they drew closer to the city. The truck grumbled, downshifting in the increased traffic, as it crossed over the Penobscot River. Seth and Sarah decided it was safe to climb up on top to look around a little.

"I have missed our home," Sarah said. The truck

traveled through the city. "We were not cut out for living in the woods. I miss the people, the noise, and the activity."

The truck rattled along State Street following the river. Old maple trees grew near the road. Their branches reached out, touching each other from both sides.

"Look at the children flying kites in Cascade Park." A warm breeze blew up from the river. "We're almost home!" Sarah said happily.

Sarah heard a swooshing sound. She looked around to see Seth clinging to a tree branch as the truck traveled down the road. "Oh, no! Nicholas, look! Seth has been swept off the truck. Help him, Nicholas!"

Nicholas looked forward instead. He saw another tree approaching with big maple leaves drooped over the road. "Sarah, we have to jump into the next tree. We have to get off this truck. It is not going to stop."

"I don't know if I can do that. It looks very dangerous. You have to help Seth," Sarah pleaded with Nicholas.

"Hold on to me and I'll jump for that branch up ahead," Nicholas said.

Sarah held tightly to Nicholas. Nicholas timed his jump as the truck passed under the branch. His paws just caught the low-hanging branch. The driver motored on, unaware he had lost his passengers.

Nicholas hung onto the branch over the roadway. Sarah held onto him with her paws around his neck. Nicholas could feel his paws slowly slipping from the branch. He didn't want to fall down into the traffic. He took a breath, leapt for the biggest maple leaf he could find, and grabbed it as he fell.

Nicholas held the leaf in both paws to catch the breeze. The wind pushed the leaf away from the road. Nicholas and Sarah landed with a thud in the grass. Seth ran up to them.

"Sarah, are you all right?" Seth asked. He helped her up. She had kept her eyes closed the whole time.

"We're home," he said.

"I'm fine, Seth. I was so worried about you." The two mice hugged.

"I'm all right, too," Nicholas said, rubbing his bruised tail. "I'll be fine."

"Thank you for rescuing me," Sarah said. "Let's go home."

"We live in the old waterworks just outside of town. We wanted a quiet place to raise our young ones. We have many mice as neighbors. They might know your cousin Francis," Seth said.

The mice traveled along the river the short distance to the waterworks. The city had built the brick buildings long ago. At one time, great pumps moved water from the river to supply the city. Many of the roofs of the old buildings had fallen in, but the brick walls still stood. The abandoned complex made an ideal community for small animals near the city, but away from the hustle and bustle of humans.

When Nicholas saw all the burrows, nests, and mice, he was sure he would find Francis, or at least he would meet someone who had heard of him. Then, he could head home to his family with the journal safe and sound at last.

Chapter Eleven

Nicholas settled in to a small space low in the brick wall. He watched young mice chase each other around old, rusted gears and over long-silent motors. Grown-up mice gossiped with each other at the openings of their nests. He could see the river sparkle and flash in the late afternoon light.

Nicholas noticed two mice on the roof beams pacing back and forth like lookouts. Nicholas approached a group of mice discussing the news of the day.

"And I heard," one mouse was saying, "that the eagles are back to stay."

"I'm not worried about the eagles," another mouse said. "They mostly eat dead fish anyway. I'm worried about the coyotes. I hear howling when the moon is full."

"The coyotes are no problem if you keep the young ones in at night. Now, I've seen a pack of weasels prowling around the neighborhood," a third mouse said. "We have to depend on ourselves for protection," the mouse went on. "We have to stick together." All the mice nodded in agreement.

"My best friend is a chipmunk," Nicholas spoke up. "I could always depend on Edward. We helped each other all the time."

"Where is he now? Is he here?" The mice looked nervously up at the two lookouts.

"No, he's not here," Nicholas said, sadly. "He had to go to his home in Massachusetts, and I haven't seen him for a long time."

"Massachusetts, you say," an old mouse said, coming up to the group. "You're not from around here, are you, young fella?"

"No, my name is Nicholas and I am here looking for my cousin Francis. He lives in Maine and he has a journal of all my family stories. Do you know him?"

"No, can't say that I do. Kind of unusual, a mouse keeping a journal, isn't it?"

Before Nicholas could answer, the two lookouts

shouted down to the others. "The muskrat is coming this way."

All the mice scattered. The grown-up mice brought the young ones into their nests, and Nicholas found himself alone on the grass-covered floor. He ducked behind an old iron pipe.

A brown, roly-poly muskrat waddled into the building. "Now I don't know why they do that," the muskrat said, shaking his head. "I've been trying to say hello for weeks. Every time they see me coming, they just skedaddle." The muskrat sat down with a sad humph.

Nicholas crept around the pipe and sniffed at the muskrat. "Why, hello there, Mr. Muskrat. How do you do? I'm Nicholas."

The muskrat nearly fell over.

"Where did you come from?" he asked, sitting up again. "Why haven't you run away like the other mice?"

"You look like you need a friend," Nicholas said. "You won't hurt me, will you?"

"Hurt you? I wouldn't hurt you. I like grass and cattails, and I love water lilies. Yes, they're sweet and tender, mmhmm." The muskrat smacked his lips at the thought. "Say, would you like to try some water lilies? I know where some are growing in a little cove on the river."

"That sounds good. I haven't had a good meal in a long time," said Nicholas.

The two animals made their way out the opening in the wall. From behind, he heard the mice in the building calling out, "Don't go with him. Are you crazy? Did you see the way he smacked his lips? That's the last we'll see of that mouse. What was his name again? Nicholas?"

The muskrat and Nicholas pushed through the tall grass down to the riverside. The muskrat pointed to a tall pine tree with a dead branch near the top.

An eagle, his head pale and beak yellow, stood tall and still. He looked down at the animals on the riverbank. His talons gripped the dead branch. Nicholas shivered.

"His name is Isaac," the muskrat said. "I bring him dead fish I find on the shore. He scared off a pack of hungry coyotes once. Do you want to meet him?"

"I don't know, he could swallow me whole," Nicholas said.

"Just wait a minute," the muskrat said. He flipped into the water. He soon popped back up dragging a fish. "This will hold the eagle's attention."

Nicholas heard a great swooping of wings. The air filled with dust and leaves. The great eagle, nearly three feet tall, stood on top of the dead fish.

"Thank you, my friend," the eagle said, in his slow careful speech. He casually tore the fish into bits as he ate.

"This is my new friend Nicholas," the muskrat said. "He's looking for his cousin somewhere in the state. Maybe you can help him."

Isaac gazed at Nicholas while he chewed. "Nicholas, do you know how big this state is? It's as big as all the other New England states put together. What makes you think you will find a little mouse in this vast state?"

"I have to find him. My family is counting on me," Nicholas said.

The eagle was picking over the bones of his dinner. "Nicholas, I will show you just how big this state is. You may change your mind about looking for your little cousin."

Before Nicholas could protest, Isaac clasped Nicholas in his great talons and leaped into the air. Even with all his strength, the eagle held Nicholas gently.

The muskrat slowly waved his paw. "Good-bye, Nicholas. Thank you for talking with me," the muskrat said as Isaac flew in a wide circle over the waterworks.

Nicholas waved back. "Thank you for your help," he said. Nicholas could see down into the roofless buildings. The mice were scurrying about, looking for places to hide. "Now, what could they be scared of?" Nicholas wondered. He looked forward as Isaac followed the river north and away from the city.

Chapter Twelve

Down at the waterworks, the mice were in hiding. A chubby little chipmunk had wandered into the same opening through which Nicholas had just left. The chipmunk called out, "Hello, is anyone around? I was told, quite specifically, I would find mice in this building."

The chipmunk held his paws on his rounded little hips and tapped a paw on the ground. "I have come a long way looking for Nicholas. I was led to believe I would find mice in this old building."

Edward heard whispers all around. "Now, really," he said. "I can hear you all making noise. Someone should just come out and speak to me."

A little mouse nose popped out of a hole in the wall. "Do you know Nicholas?" the mouse asked in a very quiet voice.

"Why, of course I know Nicholas," the chipmunk said. "He and I are great friends. I'm sure he must have mentioned me. We traveled the whole length of Massachusetts together. I have some very important news for Nicholas."

More mice came out of their hiding places. A small crowd gathered around the chipmunk. "He did mention a chipmunk friend of his," a brave mouse said.

"He said his friend's name was Everett, or Eliot, or something?" another mouse offered.

"No, I think his name was Edison." This came from a smart-looking young mouse.

"My name is Edward," the chipmunk said. "I knew you would have heard of me." Edward puffed out his chest in the way he liked to do to show how important he was. He had a real crowd around him now.

"Tell us, Edward, how did you find this place?" they asked.

Edward looked around at the eager faces. "Well, you see, it wasn't an easy journey. I've been through terrific storms. I have had to outsmart the wildest animals. I've hitched rides on trucks and trains."

Edward had the mice hooked. They sat with rapt attention listening to Edward spin more and more fantastic tales. He talked for hours. He talked until his voice gave out. A mouse offered him a sip of water in a flower petal. Edward thought he might stay here with these mice for a while.

"You have a comfortable home here," Edward said to the mice. "Perhaps I should stay here with you? It looks like you could use my protection," Edward said.

"Yes, you could stay here with us," a mouse said. "We can move you into an empty burrow right near the entrance. That way, you could always be on the lookout for wild animals."

"Wild animals, you say?" Edward asked. "Do you get very many of them around here? Maybe I should find a room a little higher up. You know, that way I can be on the lookout for trouble."

Edward made himself at home. The mice came by every day to hear stories. They didn't seem to mind that he made them up. They enjoyed the adventures, and he made them feel more secure.

As summer progressed, the muddy, wet ground around the old buildings dried out. Wintergreen, wild geraniums, and daisies came into bloom. More animals appeared along the riverside.

A playful pack of weasels turned up one day while Edward was out wandering along the river. The weasels, jumping over each other and splashing in and out of the water, discovered Edward.

"Well, who's this now?" the first weasel said.

Edward stopped in his tracks.

"He seems like he's lost," the second weasel said. "I don't remember ever seeing you before."

Edward started to back up.

"Now, see here," he said. "I'm just out for a bit of a stroll. No need for trouble."

"We've just come back from a winter down south," the third weasel said. "Do you live here now?"

"I live up the hill at the waterworks. I'll have you know I am watching out for all the mice."

"You look out for them, do you?" the first weasel said. The three weasels pressed closer to Edward. "That used to be our job."

"I certainly do. That is, they asked me to watch out for them," Edward said. "But you know, they really don't need my protection. They can look out for themselves. Or, if you three like, you can watch out for them."

"Yes, we'll do that," the weasel said.

"You know, I really need to look for my friend

Nicholas. I should be getting along," Edward said, backing away from the weasels.

"That's right, leave the mice to us," the second weasel said. He licked his lips as he spoke.

Edward turned and headed north along the river. "Yes, tell the mice I had to run along. Very important that I find Nicholas."

Edward watched the three weasels turn toward the brick buildings. "Well, there's nothing I can do about it." He shrugged and turned around. He walked along for a while, thinking about how kind the mice had been to him. They loved to hear his stories, he thought. They had given him a place to live and plenty of food. He stopped and watched the water flow back down toward the waterworks.

"My news for Nicholas will have to wait. I must help my new mice friends," Edward said aloud to his reflection in the water. "I don't know how I will help them, but I can't go on yet."

Edward started back toward the brick buildings, trying to work out how to save the mice from the weasels. He would have a real adventure to tell Nicholas when he did catch up with him, Edward thought, wherever Nicholas was in the big state of Maine.

Chapter Thirteen

Nicholas traveled far from the waterworks with the help of Isaac the bald eagle. While flying north from Bangor, Nicholas was not aware that Edward was searching for him in that city. He felt liked a caged bird, encircled in the great eagle's talons. Isaac flapped his seven-foot-long wings in slow, even strokes. They flew high over towns, cities, and long stretches of forest dotted with ponds, big lakes, and wandering rivers.

"We are headed for the great north woods," the eagle said. "It has been the home of native people for thousands of years. Loggers have worked the forests. Hunters have tracked game. Tourists and visitors of all kinds have sought out the beauty of this wild part of Maine. It has endured all of this, and yet remains wild."

Nicholas could see a tall mountain looming in the east. They steered away from it and headed for the biggest lake Nicholas had ever seen. "We are headed for Moosehead Lake," Isaac said. "This long trip has made me hungry."

Nicholas wanted to take the eagle's mind off food. From the air, Nicholas saw a great stone that looked like an animal rising out of the waters of the big lake. "What is that?" he asked, pointing down to the rock.

"That is Kineo," Isaac said. "It rises up out of the lake like a bull moose. Natives came here from many miles around in search of flint from Kineo. They made arrowheads and tools from the flint. There are signs of native settlements here from over six thousand years ago."

Isaac circled down out of the sky. He floated into a swampy area. He passed over a hillock of young cattails and deposited Nicholas. He flew to the top of a cedar tree and landed on a branch.

Nicholas looked up at the eagle. "What are we doing in this swampy place?" Nicholas had been through a flood at home. He didn't like being around so much water.

"We are waiting for my friend," Isaac said. "I am going off to the lake to fish for salmon. I'll be back."

Isaac took off, leaving Nicholas alone. It was quiet, except for the sounds of the swamp. Cicadas buzzed in the heat of the sun. A woodpecker tapped a dead tree for insects. Somewhere, something splashed over the wet ground. Nicholas swatted at a cloud of black flies.

He listened to the splashing noise move closer. The mucking sound of flat heavy feet echoed through the swamp. Nicholas tried to hide himself among the reeds. A frog leaped into the shallow water with a splash.

A mother moose appeared from around a stand of black spruce. A small calf followed close behind her. They grazed in the shallow water. The mother ducked her head down and came up dripping water from her long nose and furry chin. She munched on the tender grasses torn off at the bottom. The calf, when she came up, sputtered and coughed. She spit out some mud and swallowed the few bits of roots she had found underwater.

"Now, Phoebe, dear," the mother moose said. "I've told you many times, don't try to swallow your food when your head is underwater."

Nicholas giggled watching the young animal. The mother turned toward the noise and stood still. Phoebe tucked in close to her mother.

"I'm sorry. I didn't mean to laugh," Nicholas said.

The young calf clomped over to where Nicholas

clung to a cattail. "Hello there. Who are you? You look like you need some help," the moose asked.

"I'm Nicholas. I'm waiting for someone. I was left on this clump of grass with no way to get to dry land." He scrambled back up to the top of the cattail.

"I can help you," Phoebe said. She put her nose down close to Nicholas. He jumped on, and the young moose splashed over to higher ground near the spruce trees. The low branches of the tree nearly swept Nicholas to the ground.

"You be careful," the mother moose said. "He's just a little mouse. Maybe he's not used to such rough travel."

"Oh, I'm all right," Nicholas said. "I might be a little mouse, but I've had all kinds of adventures." Nicholas stood up as tall as he could. "I have come a long way and met many different animals in my travels."

"Are you lost?" Phoebe asked.

"Well, I don't know where I am, but I'm looking for my cousin Francis. He lives in Maine and I have to find him. An eagle named Isaac brought me up here. He wanted to show me how big this state really is."

"Moosehead Lake is big, but you should travel to Katahdin if you want to see how big the state of Maine is," the mother moose said. "I am taking Phoebe there for the rest of the summer. You can travel with us."

As the animals talked, Isaac swooped in and landed near the top of the spruce tree. The branch swayed back and forth with the great bird's weight.

79

"Hello, Isaac," the mother moose said.

"There you are, Helen," Isaac said. "I see you have found Nicholas. I set him down to wait for you."

"Nicholas is going to come to Katahdin with us," Helen said.

"Ah, very good," Isaac said. "I told this little mouse he should see for himself just how big the state of Maine is. If you take him to Katahdin, he will see."

"What is Katahdin?" Nicholas asked. "Do you think my cousin Francis will be there?"

Helen the moose looked at Isaac. "We shall see, Nicholas. We shall see. Come. It is time to get out of the midday heat." Nicholas climbed back on to Phoebe's nose.

"Your little paws tickle," Phoebe giggled, as the three animals made their way into the shade of the forest.

Chapter Fourteen

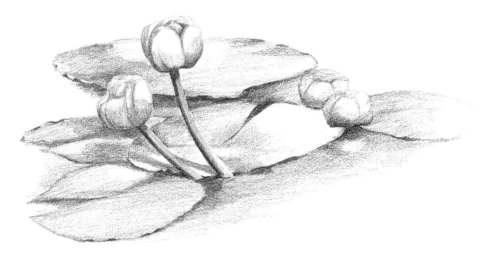

Helen and Phoebe traveled through the forests and swamps of the Moosehead Lake region. In the misty mornings, they wandered along streams or ponds, eating watercress and yellow pond lily roots. The moose would sleep through the heat of the day under great hemlocks, pine, or spruce trees.

Nicholas rode with Phoebe, telling her of his adventures in search of his family journal. He would sit atop her head, ducking under tree branches. Sometimes he would sleep between her shoulders as she walked. Nicholas thought they rolled in an uneven gait, like the deck of boat.

They came to a pond sparkling clear and bright in the sunshine. "I want to go swimming," Phoebe shouted as she splashed into the water.

"Be careful," Nicholas said, holding on to one of Phoebe's floppy ears.

The little moose paddled through the cool water with her big feet. Helen swam behind, gracefully moving her legs as if she were walking. Phoebe tried to splash Nicholas.

"Hey, I don't swim as well as you," Nicholas said.

Phoebe waded ashore. Water poured off her fur. "I feel much cooler now. How about you, Nicholas?"

"I'm fine really," Nicholas said. "At least your swim got rid of the black flies following us." Helen led them on into the woods on the far side of the pond.

In time, they made their way into Baxter State Park. The landscape became wilder. Fallen trees made it hard to travel. That night, Nicholas listened to a pack of coyotes howling. Even the big moose grew restless listening to the noise.

Helen tried to take their minds off the night by telling them about the park. "All this land, thousands and thousands of acres, were set aside by Percival Baxter to remain forever wild. This forest is just a glimpse of what New England was like at one time. Black bear, bald eagles, and moose, like us, roamed the forests and rivers."

The coyotes howled again. "Coyotes have not always been here in Maine," Helen said, looking toward the noise. "They moved in from other states as their territories there were developed."

"They seem to be getting closer to us," Phoebe said, trying to snuggle closer to her mother.

"You stay near to me, Phoebe," her mother said in the dark. "Those coyotes won't bother you as long as I'm nearby."

Phoebe folded her long legs tightly under her body and leaned against her mother's side. Nicholas tried to look through the darkness. A twig snapped nearby. Nicholas hopped up on top of Phoebe's head.

"I hear something out there," Phoebe said. "What is it, mother?"

"Shh, Phoebe," Helen whispered. "Lay still. Whatever it is, it is still out there." They heard branches swishing in the dark. All three animals sensed someone watching. "You stay here with Nicholas, Phoebe. I'm going to see what is out there." There was very little in the forests of Maine that could scare an animal as big as a moose.

Nicholas, however, was much smaller than a moose. He stayed close to Phoebe. The coyotes howled again, much closer this time. Nicholas and Phoebe listened to animals running through the forest. It sounded like Helen smashing through the trees. The coyotes barked and yipped in the night. Phoebe stood up, ready to run after her mother.

"Now hold on, Phoebe," Nicholas said. "Your mother wants us to stay right here. She'll be all right."

"What if I can help her?" Phoebe said. "What if those coyotes get her?"

"I bet your mother is leading the animals away to keep you safe," Nicholas said. "She'll be back soon." Nicholas hoped this was true. He heard a moose bellow off in the distance.

"I can't wait here," Phoebe said. She crashed off into the dark, calling for her mother.

"No, Phoebe, it isn't safe," Nicholas said. It was too late. Nicholas was alone. He knew he should stay where he was. He didn't know how he would ever find either moose in such a big forest. The sounds of the night were all around. An owl hooted from behind him. Nicholas jumped at the noise. He took off into the trees. He had no choice but to try to catch up with Phoebe.

He ran over the pine-needle-covered forest floor as fast as a little mouse could go. Using his whiskers, he tried to sense a path around pinecones, under fallen branches, and through clumps of wildflowers. His heart beat fast in his chest. In places, the ground was stony and steep. The owl seemed to be following him. It hooted again. He jumped, tumbled down the sloping ground, and rolled off a short ledge.

Nicholas fell through the air. He landed with a thud in a pile of rocks. He was sore, tired, and scared. He continued to breathe heavily. One leg was stuck in the rocks and his head hurt. The owl flew by overhead without seeing Nicholas in the shadows. He was safe for now.

Nicholas was alone and lost, deep in the woods of Maine. He had no idea how to get his leg unstuck. He didn't know where he was, or what had happened to his friends. He lay on his side, snuggled next to the rock, looking up through the trees at the stars shining down fiercely from the sky. In time, Nicholas dozed off, passing the night restlessly.

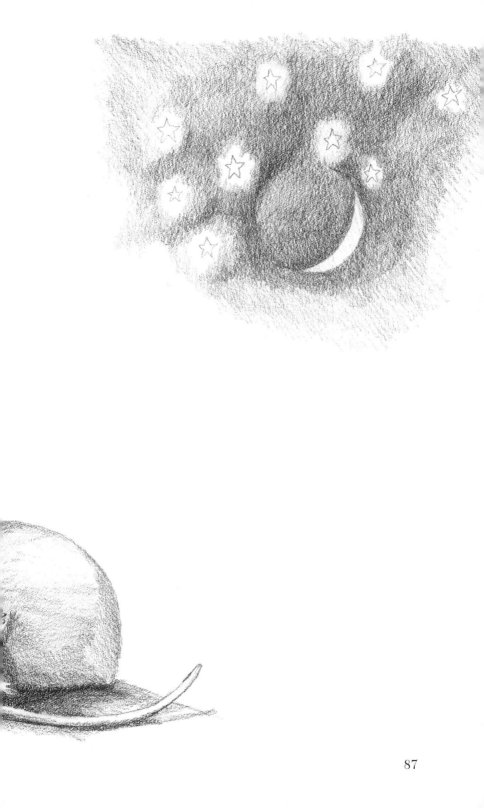

Chapter Fifteen

Nicholas awoke with the sun shining through the trees. A warm breeze rustled the tassels of the big pines. A chipmunk stood looking at him from the top of the rock pile. Nicholas tried to focus on the brown furry animal. His head hurt from falling on the rocks.

"Edward," Nicholas said. "Is it really you? I'm stuck. Can you help me?"

The chipmunk scrambled down to Nicholas, dragging a long stick.

"Are you all right?" the chipmunk asked.

"Edward, it's me." Nicholas squinted with blurry eyes. He tried to get up, but his leg was stuck under the rock. "Ouch, that really hurts." Nicholas fell back down. "What are you doing, Edward?"

The chipmunk had stuck one end of the stick under the rock holding Nicholas's leg. The other end stood out like a lever. The chipmunk, standing at the top of the rock pile, eyed the distance to the stick. He jumped. "I'm not Edward," the chipmunk said, landing on the end of the stick. The stick popped the rock loose and Nicholas was free.

"My name is Thomas. I saw you pinned under the rock and I wanted to help," he said.

"What happened to Helen and Phoebe? Are they all right?" Nicholas sat up and held his sore leg with his paw.

"Yes, they are fine. Helen led the coyotes far away. She came back in time to find her daughter, lost and wandering down a stream. They told me that you were somewhere about," the chipmunk said. "They said to say good-bye. They don't want to stay around if the coyotes come back. They made me promise to help you out of these rocks."

"I thought you were Edward, my friend," Nicholas said sadly. Nicholas told Thomas his story. He started with the big flood at home and kept on talking for an hour. When Nicholas finished, the two animals sat for a while in silence.

At last, Thomas stood up. "That is an amazing story, Nicholas. Isaac is right, Maine is a big state, but I think I can help you. I know a place in the state where mice like to live. There are lots of foods, barns to make nests in, and not many people."

Nicholas jumped up. "Where is this place, Thomas? Can we go there today?" Nicholas asked. His leg throbbed with pain. He sat back down, holding his leg again.

"I don't think you will be able to travel for a little while, Nicholas. You can stay here with me. I'll take care of you," Thomas said. "Then I will show you where you might find your cousin."

Nicholas spent some time on the side of the great mountain called Katahdin by the natives. He rested his leg. Thomas brought him wild oats and pinecones to eat. In time, Nicholas was up and about again. The two wandered on the mountainside.

They liked to race up and down among the hemlocks. They slid downhill on the bed of old evergreen needles. They tried to see how far each could slide. Thomas had gotten a long running start and slid all the way to the base of a gnarled old tree. A nuthatch hanging upside down clung to the bark and watched him pass.

Nicholas took his turn. He backed up the shady hillside and took off. He jumped on his belly and slid down the slope. The short hemlock needles sprayed out from either side. Nicholas laughed when he saw that he would pass his friend. As he passed Thomas, an old spruce grouse waddled into his path. She was pecking at the ground, gathering hemlock seeds.

"Watch out!" Thomas shouted to Nicholas.

"Watch out!" Nicholas said, too late, to the grouse.

BANG—Nicholas crashed into her side. The grouse, stout, compact, and low to the ground, wasn't hurt.

"I should say, you should really watch yourself, young man," the old grouse said. "I suggest you choose more carefully where you go sliding."

Nicholas bounced off her and came to a stop, upside down with his tail over his head. "Oh, my," Nicholas said, still upside down. He flopped over. "Are you all right? I am so sorry. Did I hurt you?"

"I," the grouse responded, "am fine. You, on the other hand, seem to be the worse for wear."

Small hemlock needles, dust, and bits of pine pitch covered Nicholas from head to tail. "Oh, no," Nicholas said, brushing himself off. "I'm really fine."

Thomas skidded down to a stop next to Nicholas. "Nicholas, you beat me by a mile. That was awesome." He looked at the grouse. "Hello, Henrietta, I hope you are all right. This is my friend Nicholas. He's from Massachusetts and he's looking for a mouse cousin of his."

"From Massachusetts you say, humph. I might have guessed as much," Henrietta said. "Mouse families are quite large. I am not surprised to hear you are related to mice in Maine."

"I told him he might find his cousin in the county," Thomas said. "You know, Henrietta, there are plenty of farms in the county. Mice just love farms."

"They certainly do. I will even offer to take him part of the way if you two are through with your sliding games."

"You would do that?" Nicholas said. "Even after I ran into you and all?"

"Precisely because you ran into me, young mouse," Henrietta said. "If I help you, I have less chance of being hit again. I will take you to Chimney Pond. From there, I am sure you can find a way north."

Nicholas, grateful to his friend Thomas, said his good-byes and climbed up onto the spruce grouse's back. In a great flurry of wings and a spray of dust, Nicholas and Henrietta were off.

Chapter Sixteen

Henrietta flew among the low branches of the hemlock trees. She dodged and weaved over and under the hanging boughs. She found a path faster than Nicholas could guess which way she was going next. He hunkered down on her back and tried not to watch.

Henrietta flew higher up the mountainside. The trees thinned out. Sharp granite boulders stuck out in her path. They eventually came to a pond. Henrietta stopped to rest near its shore. She drank from the clear cold water. Nicholas sat on a stone. He looked up at the great mountain ridge of many sharp peaks.

"I have brought you as far as I can," Henrietta said. "This is Chimney Pond. Baxter Peak and Mount Katahdin are before you. Aroostook County lies to the north over this mountain."

"How will I get over that mountain?" Nicholas asked. "If I started now, it would take me weeks to hike up there myself."

"Now, Nicholas, I am sure you are a smart young mouse. Many hikers make their way up the mountain from here. Perhaps you can get a ride with one of them."

"I don't know," Nicholas said.

"Well, while you are resting, perhaps you will think of something. I would like to get back to my snug nest now. Good-bye, Nicholas." The grouse rustled off, without as much as waiting for Nicholas to say good-bye.

Nicholas watched hikers arrive carrying backpacks and tents. They set up their camps under the trees. He made his way to a stand of aspens near the pond and made a nest of leaves. Clouds sailed in from over the top of the mountain. A rumble of thunder echoed around the mountain range.

Nicholas covered himself with the leaves, quaking at the approaching storm. Fat raindrops fell from the sky. It grew dark and cold. The wind whistled down the mountainside and the rain pelted the pond. Nicholas dozed off-and-on until late into the night.

He awoke with a start. He could not tell the time. It was still deep, dark night, but Nicholas sensed something moving along the shore. He thought maybe a hiker was trying to rescue a tent blown away in the storm. He could see someone coming his way. He buried himself under the leaves again.

The figure stood on the edge of the aspen trees. A wave of cold wind rustled the leaves. The lightning flashed and the thunder rumbled. "Who are you, and why have you come to my mountain?" the figure asked. Wings grew out of his back and his feet were like an eagle's talons.

"I am Nicholas," the mouse said, standing up as tall as he could. "I only want to get over the mountain."

"I am Pamola. I live among the clouds, high on this mountain. I protect the mountain and control who can climb to the summit," the figure said. "I bring the thunder and cold."

Nicholas looked at the figure standing in shadow. "I am looking for my cousin. He has a journal of our family history. I have to find a way over this mountain to continue my journey north."

Nicholas could not see the figure well in the dark and rain. He was afraid, but he needed a way over the mountain. The figure that seemed half-man and half-animal picked up Nicholas. In the blink of an eye, Nicholas found himself soaring through the storm. He was not wet from the rain nor cold from the wind. He floated through the clouds, held securely by the strange figure. He closed his eyes.

Nicholas awoke in the early morning amid a forest of fir trees. The storm had passed. Warblers and wrens sang among the trees. Katahdin's peak was clear of clouds and behind Nicholas. He had made it over the mountain. He wasn't sure who had helped him the previous night. It didn't matter. He could continue on his way north.

Nicholas traveled on alone. He wandered through the deep forest. He saw no one for days at a time. He stopped to eat when he found food, and he slept when he was tired. The sun rarely peeked through to the forest floor.

He came to a stream that babbled over its rocky bed. He followed it along the gently sloping ground. He could see fields and farmlands ahead. A family of white-tailed deer browsed on the edge of the field. One deer raised its head while the others fed. Nicholas stumbled out of the forest, blinking in the bright morning sun.

"Hello, little mouse," the deer said. "Come and share some of this fine grass with us."

Nicholas felt weak and shaky after being in the forest for so long. He sat on the ground near the deer and nibbled the grass. "Where am I?" he asked in a soft voice.

"You are in the county," the deer said. "This is Aroostook County, the very top of the state of Maine."

"I have been traveling for days alone in the forest. I can't believe I made it all the way here," Nicholas said.

He looked out at the landscape. The fields rolled on and on, like great waves out on the ocean. Low crops grew fresh and green in patches as far as Nicholas could see. A red barn and a cluster of buildings stood out on a distant rise.

"Well, I see a farm. And, as Henrietta said, 'Where there's a farm, there are bound to be mice,'" Nicholas said to the deer. The deer had walked on. They were within the shade of the forest trees. "I guess I had better start walking," Nicholas shrugged. He made a path through the field and hoped he would find Francis at last.

Chapter Seventeen

Nicholas walked through the big field heading toward the barn. He had grown up on a farm. He knew he should keep under cover as much as possible. There was always a hawk, an owl, or a fox on the lookout for a mouse out in the open. Nicholas nibbled the stalk of a plant growing in the big field. The sunlight made the leaves shimmer green and white.

Overhead, a Cooper's hawk made wide circles, scanning the fields. Nicholas watched the bird as he ate. He tried to keep low and out of sight. He peeked out from behind a broad leaf and could not see the bird. It must have moved on, Nicholas thought. He continued on his way toward the barn.

He was sure the mice in the barn would have news of his cousin. He was thinking how nice it would be to be among friends again when he felt a strong whoosh of wind and felt the talons of the hawk brush by his head. Nicholas hunkered down and ran.

The hawk took another dive. It trapped Nicholas's tail against the ground. Nicholas pulled with all his might. He tumbled free and ran off again. The hawk lifted up with his wings and was ready to strike the running mouse, but Nicholas had disappeared. The hawk flapped into the air, tilting his head side-to-side, looking for the brown mouse in the green field.

Nicholas was underground. He rolled to a stop against a furry little animal. "Oh, I beg your pardon," Nicholas said, sitting up and shaking the dirt out of his fur. "I seem to have stumbled into your tunnel."

The meadow vole turned around. He was startled but not surprised. "Quite all right, quite all right," the vole replied. "Let me guess: the Cooper's hawk chased you underground. It happens all the time."

"I'm so glad your tunnel was here. I'm Nicholas. I was headed for the barn when the hawk surprised me."

"How do you do? I'm Rodney. Are you hurt, Nicholas?"

"I think I'm fine. My tail got a scrape, but I'll be all right." Nicholas rubbed at his tail.

"I believe you will," Rodney said, looking at Nicholas. "Some mice have not made out so well against the Cooper's hawk," Rodney said. "The young ones forget to stay under cover in the fields. I try to remind them, but …," the meadow vole trailed off.

"You seem to have made out all right. Follow me. I'll take you to the barn in the only safe way there is to travel around here—underground." The vole took off down the tunnel, knocking dirt from the walls as he moved. Nicholas tried to keep up. He coughed and sneezed in the dust.

The vole talked as he traveled. "I have tunnels and runs all over this farm. I can travel anywhere in this field of broccoli without worrying about the hawks. I've told the mice they can use my tunnels any time, but they have their own way of doing things."

"Do you know many mice?" Nicholas asked. "I've been searching everywhere for my cousin Francis. He has my family journal and I need to find him."

"A journal, did you say?" Rodney stopped in his tracks. He turned around to look at Nicholas. "I do know a mouse who told me he has stories about his family that go quite far back in history. He was an interesting young mouse." Rodney looked at Nicholas for a moment. "He looked a bit like you, Nicholas."

"That must be him," Nicholas said. Jumping up, he bumped his head on the roof of the tunnel. "When was the last time you saw him? Do you know where he is now?" Nicholas had been searching for his cousin so long. Now, Nicholas was talking to someone who actually knew his cousin Francis.

"Slow down now, Nicholas. I said I spoke to him a while ago. I haven't seen him for some time." Rodney could see the excitement ebb from Nicholas's face.

"I know someone who will know where Francis is. Let's get to the barn."

Nicholas followed Rodney. They ran along among the roots of the broccoli plants. The tunnel floor started to rise. The two animals popped above ground along a line of spruce trees growing next to a long, low barn built into the ground.

"This is the potato storage," Rodney said. "This barn is kept cool by being half underground and shaded by the line of trees. After harvest time, this barn will be full of potatoes. Now it is mostly empty. The final barrels from last year's harvest are being shipped out."

Nicholas and Rodney climbed the grassy slope at one end of the barn and squeezed under the loose-fitting door. Inside, the barn was quiet and cool. Tiny shafts of light, showing dust in the air, angled to the ground. The last barrels of potatoes stood in a row, waiting for a truck.

All Nicholas wanted was to find out about his cousin. He wanted to meet whoever it was that had information about Francis. "When the sun sets, Audrey will be back," Rodney stated. The pair settled in to wait for Audrey to return.

Chapter Eighteen

Nicholas watched the slant of sunlight slowly settle lower and lower. The big potato barn grew dark. Crickets sent their tune out into the dusk. Rodney snoozed next to Nicholas. Occasionally, Nicholas thought he heard someone approaching the barn.

The sun sank below the horizon. Soon a bird came flitting through the narrow space between the doors. She sang out, "Kvik-kvik-kvik." She looped up toward the roof, swung low toward Nicholas and Rodney, and then landed on a mud nest built high up on the side of the barn.

"Good evening, Audrey," Rodney said. "How was your day?"

"Hello, Rodney," Audrey said, in her high soft voice. "I've been down by the river. I do so like the insects that fly over the river."

"Audrey, this is my friend Nicholas. He has come a long way looking for his cousin Francis. You know

Francis, I believe? He was always going on about his family stories and that journal."

"I remember Francis," Audrey said. "He read to me from it many times. There were stories of long ago. There were stories from when Maine was still part of Massachusetts. There were even stories of his mouse family traveling with explorers from the first colony in Massachusetts to Maine to trade with the natives."

"You know Francis!" Nicholas jumped up, interrupting Audrey. "I've been looking up and down the state for him. Where is he? Does he live in this barn?"

"Now, Nicholas, I haven't talked with Francis for some time. I was telling about his stories," Audrey started to say.

"I know and I'm sorry, but when did you last see him?" Nicholas asked.

"Last summer—he was going to the Potato Blossom Festival in Fort Fairfield."

"Fort Fairfield? Where's that?" Nicholas sat down with a bump. His excitement at nearly finding his cousin quickly disappeared.

"Oh, it's only up the road a piece," Audrey said.

"How long will it take to travel to Fort Fairfield?" Nicholas asked. He was ready to start right now.

"Hold on, Nicholas," Rodney said. "Remember the hawk outside. He won't let you travel all the way to Fort Fairfield."

"Rodney is right," Audrey said. "I will go. I'll ask around and find out what I can. You stay here with

Rodney. When I come back I'll bring any news."

"Well," Nicholas sighed, "I guess I can wait a while longer."

"There you go, Nicholas," Rodney said. "I'll show you around the place tomorrow. Let Audrey get some rest tonight."

The next morning Nicholas woke up and saw that Audrey had already left. Rodney, who had slept soundly nearby, was also gone. Nicholas lay where he was. He had not slept well the night before. He was anxious to find his cousin and get home to his family and their own farm.

"Good morning, good morning!" Rodney said, waddling into the barn. "What a beautiful day, Nicholas. We have lots to see and do today. Up, up, up."

"What do you mean, we have lots of things to do today?" Nicholas asked. "I thought I would wait here for Audrey to come back."

"Nonsense, nonsense, Nicholas," Rodney said. He tugged at Nicholas's paw, dragging him up from his bed. "We have to go visit the cows. There is plenty of leftover milk for us. Then, we have to check on the honeybees out by the potato fields. They always have interesting things to talk about."

Nicholas and Rodney crossed the barnyard. The hawk was nowhere around. The cows, waiting to go outside, shuffled their feet when the small animals came into the barn.

"*Bon matin, monsieur* Rodney," a black-and-white

cow called Jacques said. "Who is this *petit* mouse, eh?"

"*Bon jour*, Jacques. This is my friend Nicholas. I wanted to show him the barn."

"*Bon jour*, Nicholas," the French-speaking cow said. "I think you will find some fresh milk in that dish, eh? It is sweet today."

Nicholas and Rodney helped themselves to the milk. "It was nice of the farmer to put this out for us," Nicholas said.

"Oh, he did not put that out for you, *petit* mouse. No, that is for *le chat*, eh?" Jacques said.

"What does he mean, *le chat*?" Nicholas asked.

Rodney wiped his fuzzy face. "*Le chat* means 'the cat' in French. These are cows from Quebec, in Canada. Everyone there speaks French."

"*Oui, c'est vrai*—that is correct," Jacques said. "I am French-Canadian, eh? *Voilá, monsieur. Le chat est ici, maintenant.*"

Rodney said, "The cat is here now."

Nicholas and Rodney looked up at the same time. A big Maine coon cat strolled down the center aisle of the barn. The cat saw Rodney and Nicholas. Everyone started to run. The cows mooed.

"This way," Rodney said. He led Nicholas along the cows' stalls. They dodged under cows' legs and tails. The cat gained on them all the time. Rodney ducked into a hole in the wall and Nicholas followed. The cat slid to a halt next to the wall.

"*Au revoir, mes amis,*" Jacques called out, laughing at the chaos. "*Bon voyage, petit* mouse."

Rodney and Nicholas came out into the barnyard. The cat could not fit through the hole and had given up the chase. They were ready to congratulate each other when Audrey flew back from her trip.

"Audrey," Rodney said, "we were not expecting you for hours. What happened?"

"Did you find Francis?" Nicholas asked quickly.

"That is why I am back so soon," Audrey said. "I have news. You have to get going right away, Nicholas. You don't have any time to waste. I'll explain everything. Hurry and follow me." Audrey flew toward the potato barn. Nicholas could not imagine why he had to hurry so. He only knew he wanted to find his cousin and perhaps Audrey would help.

Chapter Nineteen

Audrey flew in great arcs over the barnyard. Nicholas and Rodney tried to follow as best they could. She urged them to hurry. "Come along, you two," she said. She flew back to them. "The farmhands are loading the truck now. This is their last trip until next spring."

Nicholas looked up at the bird. "Last trip where?"

"They are delivering the final load of potatoes to Bath and Portland. If you hurry, you can catch a ride."

"Why do I want to go to those places? Is my cousin there?"

"Nicholas, don't ask questions now," Rodney said. He huffed and puffed a little. He wasn't used to traveling at a bird's pace. "If Audrey says you need to get on that truck, then she must have a good reason for saying it."

Audrey said, "I talked to a couple of mice at Fort Fairfield. They knew Francis. He lived with them during last year's festival. He headed south. They said Francis was upset by something."

"What could it be?" Nicholas asked. "Was it something in the journal?"

"They didn't know, but Francis headed south and this truck is your best chance to travel in that direction."

Audrey landed on a fence post. Nicholas and Rodney hid in the tall grass near the base of the post. They could see the truck in the doorway of the storage barn. The farmhands were rolling barrels up a ramp onto the back of the truck.

"Wait here," Audrey, said as she flew toward the barn. She swooped into the barn, circling over the men's heads. "Keet-keet-keet," she said. She dove between them, dodging their waving arms.

"You get along now," one man said. He ducked his head as Audrey circled around.

"Shoo, bird," the other man said. "We won't bother your nest."

Audrey kept up her flying. The men moved away from the truck. She flew in circles, further and further away. "Now get along," the second man said, following the bird out the barn door. Audrey let the men chase her away from the barn.

"Quick, Nicholas, get up that ramp and hide among the barrels. The men will be back soon," Audrey said, over her wing.

Nicholas ran for the wooden ramp. Just as he made a move to cross the open space from the post to the barn, he heard the sharp sound of the Cooper's hawk's cry. He was back and looking for Nicholas and Rodney.

The two animals tried to keep the post between them and the hawk. They knew Audrey couldn't keep the men away for long. "We are going to need some help," Nicholas said. "That hawk won't leave us alone long enough for me to get on the truck before the men come back."

The men had already given up chasing Audrey and were heading back to the truck.

"We are running out of time," Nicholas said.

The cow barn door rumbled open as the men passed. The cows were heading out of the barn on their way to the pasture. The mooing cows surrounded the men.

"Quick, Nicholas, run under the cows. The hawk won't be able to get at you," Rodney said.

"*Bon jour. Mon pauve ti bête.* My poor little thing," Jacques said. "You are caught by that post, are you not? *Allez vous*, come with me," he said.

The cow sauntered along. Nicholas stayed beneath the cow as it passed the potato barn. He ran up the ramp, into the truck, and hid behind a big round barrel of potatoes.

"Au revoir, again, *mon petit ami*," Jacques called as the herd continued its walk to the pasture.

"*Merci*, Jacques," Nicholas called, trying out a bit of French on the cow.

"You are quick to learn, little mouse. Good-bye."

The hawk wheeled off in search of an easier breakfast.

The men came back. Audrey was flying high in the sky, far out of their reach. Rodney waved goodbye to Nicholas from behind the fence post, then he ducked down one of his nearby tunnels. That was the last Nicholas saw of him. The men slammed the tailgate shut.

The two men got in the truck, bounced out of the barnyard, and out to the main road. Nicholas, in the back of the truck, looked up in the sky. Audrey circled overhead. "Good luck finding your cousin, Nicholas." Nicholas waved as the truck bumped along the patched tar road.

Traveling south, Nicholas thought about his cousin. He wondered what made Francis want to leave. What upset him so? Nicholas would have to wait to find his cousin and ask him.

The truck traveled along Route One until they came to the interstate. The old farm truck rattled and hummed, trying to keep up with fast-moving traffic. From atop a barrel, Nicholas looked backward out of the truck. He thought about all the places he had seen so far and wondered where this old truck was going to stop next.

Chapter Twenty

The truck arrived at Dover-Foxcroft, a town on the Piscataquis River in the center of the state. The men stopped the truck in front of a feed and grain store to make a delivery. An old yellow wooden building perched over the river in the center of town. From an open side door, Nicholas could smell hay, grass seed, dried herbs, and spices. It made him hungry.

The men set up the ramp and rolled two barrels off the truck. Nicholas kept out of sight. The men came out of the store before Nicholas could decide whether he should get off the truck or not. They walked off to a diner for lunch.

Nicholas decided it was safe to get off the truck. The men would be busy eating for a while. He made his way down the ramp and sniffed around for his own lunch.

The door led into a storeroom. There were crates and sacks full of seed of all kinds. Nicholas could hardly decide where to start. A family of chipping sparrows, inside on the cement floor, pecked at some spilled grass seed.

"Welcome little mouse, there is plenty for everyone," the mother sparrow said.

"Hi, I'm Nicholas. I am so very hungry!" he said. Nicholas ran up and helped himself to a mouthful of seeds. He talked with his mouth full. "I don't have much time to eat. I have to watch that truck outside. When the men come back, I need to be on the truck."

"We can watch it for him, Mom," one young bird said. She fluttered up to the mother bird. The second young bird joined them. "We can go outside by ourselves and watch for the truck drivers for him."

"Please, Mom, let us do it! We're big enough to do it ourselves," she said.

"Well, all right. Just be careful," the mother bird said.

"You two stay together," the father bird called, eating his own meal.

"Listen to your father," the mother sparrow said. "Stay near each other, and call us when the driver leaves the diner."

The two young birds flew through the door. They

settled on the sidewalk next to the truck. They pecked about under an elm tree, looking for something to eat and feeling very important.

"It is very nice of you to help me out," Nicholas said. "There is so much food here." Nicholas moved from one kind of seed to another. He moved quickly toward the back of the storeroom.

"Now watch out, Nicholas," the mother sparrow called. In his excitement, he didn't notice an old rusty mousetrap, baited long ago with peanut butter, tucked among the sacks.

Nicholas swept by the trap as he nibbled his way back into the storeroom. His tail triggered the trap. Because it was old, the spring closed slowly, but it caught Nicholas by the tail. He let out a high squeak. He took off running, dragging the trap behind him. It hurt so much. He ran between two crates of corn seed. The trap wedged tightly between the crates.

Nicholas couldn't move forward or backward. He pulled on his tail, trying to free it. Finally, he sat down and cried. "What am I going to do?" he asked aloud. He squeaked and scratched, trying to free himself from the trap. The mother bird heard him and flew over to Nicholas.

"Oh, my! There are old traps all over this building. I think the clerks in the store have forgotten about many of them," she said to Nicholas. Just then, the two young birds flew in, all out of breath.

"They're back, they're back!" the birds said together.

"We were watching, really we were. The drivers just showed up and got into the truck."

"Oh, no, my ride," Nicholas said. He tugged on his tail again. "Ouch, ouch!" he said. "Oh, that hurts." He sat down again. Outside, they heard the truck engine trying to start. The old truck sputtered and sputtered.

"I don't have much time," Nicholas said. "That is my ride south. I have to get out of here."

"Please, hurry. I couldn't bear it if you missed your ride because of me," one of the young birds said. She started to cry. The truck engine outside continued to cough and bark smoke.

"Now don't cry," the other bird said. "It will make me cry." She started up with her sister.

"Girls, please, I'm trying to think," the father bird said. He sat on his perch on the crate and did nothing. Everyone else scurried about. There was a great deal of noise and fuss. The door into the store opened and a human voice said, "Go see what all that racket is about." A springer spaniel bounded into the storeroom. The truck engine finally started and revved up. All the animals cried out.

The young dog saw the mouse and birds flitting about. He bounded into the room barking and slobbering. The excitable dog crashed into the crates where Nicholas was stuck. The crates tumbled over, spilling corn all over the floor. The dog skidded on the corn, his big puppy paws flapping on the floor. He hit the trap and it flew into the air. Nicholas was free!

Nicholas ran for the outside door. The truck was rolling away from the sidewalk. "I'm not going to make it," Nicholas shouted.

The mother and father sparrow flew after Nicholas, holding a bit of bailing twine between them. Nicholas jumped and held on to the twine. The two birds flew into the air over the truck. Nicholas let go, landing with a thump in the back.

The young birds flew out of the store sniffing. "Good-bye, little mouse," the two birds waved. Nicholas waved back. His heart beat rapidly in his chest. He was glad to be out of that town and on his way again.

Chapter Twenty One

There was another small room in the back of the grain and feed store. It had a big glass window that looked out over the river and a dusty old desk in one corner. A brown, furry chipmunk came out of the small room. He rubbed his eyes and yawned.

"What was that ruckus?" he asked. He blinked and stretched. "I have been trying to sleep," he said to the sparrows. "I awoke to the strangest sounds. Was that spaniel after you?"

"No," the mother sparrow said. "There was a young mouse. We could have used your help. He caught his tail in a trap."

"Now, I can't help every mouse who finds himself in a trap. After all, how are they going to learn about such dangers if they can't get themselves out of trouble occasionally? Besides, Rachel may need my help."

"Edward," a very silky voice called from the storage room. "I need your help."

Edward's ears perked up. "I'm on my way, my pet. What can I do for you?" he asked, scampering back into the room. He found the red squirrel sitting in a sunny spot on the floor, looking up at a pile of crates. The sun made her red fur shine.

"Edward, my dear. Will you get me some of those walnuts? I can't reach the top crate."

"Certainly, my pet," Edward said. He looked up at the poorly stacked crates. "Are you sure you want walnuts? I could find you some nice peanuts lower down."

"Oh, Edward, I had my heart set on walnuts. I suppose I could find someone else to get them for me if you don't think you can do it."

"Don't be silly, Rachel, dear. Of course I will get them," Edward said. He looked again at the tall stack of crates. The top one marked "whole walnuts" hung out over the edge of the box below it.

"Why, I've climbed to more dangerous spots before," Edward said, as he hopped onto the first crate. "Did I tell you how I outfoxed a pack of weasels down in Bangor?"

Rachel sighed and covered her mouth with a paw as she yawned. "Yes, dear, several times now."

Edward continued, "The weasels were intent on making mischief with a community of mice. I was outnumbered four-to-one," he started. "I knew I had to gain the high ground." Edward continued to climb up the boxes as he described his battle. He swung his arms this way and that as he talked. The whole stack swayed.

"Edward, be careful. You are going to knock the crates on top of me."

"Nonsense, my dear. I am perfectly safe," Edward said. He jumped to the top box. "The weasels had made their way into the building where the mice live. Of course the mice looked to me to save them," Edward continued.

"Yes, dear," Rachel said absently. She was examining her fur in the sunlight. "Do you think my fur is auburn or more of a strawberry blond color?" she asked Edward.

"I had to think fast. The weasels had half a dozen mice trapped in a corner. Well, the only thing I could do was swoop down on an old lamp chain. I screamed and crashed into the whole lot of those weasels." Edward was demonstrating the pose he used to bowl over the weasels. Rachel's question distracted him. The crates were swaying back and forth now. "What did you say about your fur?" he asked, looking down at her.

As he looked down, the crates leaned far to one side and tumbled to the floor. Edward screeched and leaped. Rachel screamed and ran. The boxes crashed to the floor, spilling nuts and seeds all over. Edward landed in a heap on a pile of sunflower seeds. A walnut shell clunked down and landed on his head like a helmet. Rachel laughed.

"That will protect you next time you need to fight some weasels," Rachel said. "I told you to be careful. Are you all right?"

Edward shook his head. He felt a little shaken, but not hurt.

The sparrow family came in after hearing the goings-on. "What a day it has been. First we had little Nicholas and his trapped tail, and now you, Edward."

Edward stood up. He pulled the walnut shell off his head. "Did you say Nicholas? I have been traveling all over this state looking for Nicholas. Why didn't you tell me he was just here?" Edward said.

"You never told us you were looking for Nicholas. This red squirrel seemed to occupy all of your time."

"Yes, well, Rachel seemed to need my help. I guess I just forgot about finding Nicholas. Where did he go?"

"He headed south on a truck with potatoes. I think they are headed for Portland," the mother sparrow said.

"Well, I must get to him. I know where his cousin Francis is. I can help him find his cousin. How can I get to Portland?" Edward asked.

"What about me?" Rachel asked. "Who is going to look after me?"

"Now, Rachel, you really don't need my help," Edward said. "My friend Nicholas has been searching for his cousin a long time and I know where he is."

Rachel had already stopped listening to Edward. She was brushing out her fur after all the excitement.

"Edward, a Moosehead furniture truck goes to Portland once a week. I bet you can get a ride with one of them," the mother sparrow said. Edward bounded out the door of the feed and grain store.

"I'll get on one of those trucks and catch up with Nicholas. I hope he has been all right without me," Edward said to the sparrow. He ran down the street and over to the Moosehead furniture factory, looking for his own ride south.

Chapter Twenty Two

Nicholas rattled along in the back of the truck heading south. The landscape was changing from trees, fields, and farms to stores, stoplights, and traffic. The truck got off the highway in the Kennebec River town of Bath.

The driver stopped to talk to a guard at a gate. Then the truck rolled into a busy shipyard. A sign over the gate read "Bath Iron Works." Ships and shipyards seemed like a good place to look for his cousin, Nicholas thought. He looked around at a very busy scene.

Two tall red-and-white cranes lifted ship parts high in the air. Workers in hard hats, carrying tools on their shoulders, hurried about. Sparks from welders sprayed the ground. Trucks and forklifts carrying strangely shaped metal parts crisscrossed paths all over the yard.

Nicholas wandered down the sloping ground to the river. Two gray sharp-bowed Navy ships floated at the dock. Long heavy lines swept up, holding the ships in place. The ships looked forbidding and off limits.

He headed for a quiet section of the shipyard. A quiet marsh struggled against the development of the busy shipyard. Nicholas sat on the bank of a small stream that drained the marsh. He was tired and lost and had no one to turn to for help.

The cattails rustled and shivered. A very big, very old, very grumpy-looking raccoon popped out of the reeds. He blinked at Nicholas. "I hope you're not thinking of moving to this marsh," the raccoon said. "There's little enough room for us here without other animals moving in," he said.

"I'm not looking for a place to live," Nicholas said. "I'm looking for my cousin Francis. I've been all over this state and I can't find him anywhere."

"I don't know any mouse named Francis. I know a mouse named Fred. His family lived in the shipyard. Haven't seen them since the river otters moved to town. The otters came over from Day's Ferry. Their family goes a way back, to when Bath built wooden ships."

"I've traveled all over the state. I don't know what to do," Nicholas said.

"When I have a question I can't answer, I ask Oscar," the old raccoon said. "If you want to find him, he's down the river at the museum. Ask for a gray squirrel named Oscar."

The raccoon took a breath and started in again. "Yes, now, I know a few things about this city. There was a muskrat family, lived over in Woolwich, came to town for every ship launching. They built some big ships in those days. Anyway, the muskrats got into the hold of the ship at the launching. By the time they found their way on deck again, the ship was halfway to China." The raccoon chuckled.

"The museum is down the river, you were saying?" Nicholas interrupted. "I'll see what I can find out there." Nicholas hurried off.

The raccoon shrugged. "Youngsters just don't want to hear about the old days," he said.

Nicholas could see old wooden ships and a big brick building on the banks of the river nearby. He wandered onto the museum grounds. It was much quieter, but still Nicholas didn't know where to turn.

"I figured you would need my help," Nicholas heard from behind him. The old raccoon waddled out of the marsh at the edge of the museum. "Oscar doesn't get out much anymore. Kind of keeps to himself, up in the old boat-building shed. I know the back way in, follow me."

The raccoon went around to the back of a building. A pile of cordwood was stacked against the wall. There were also some garbage barrels. "Sometimes I can find a pretty decent meal in there," he said in passing.

"Hop up there," the raccoon said, pointing to the firewood. "You can climb in through the window."

One of the windowpanes was broken. Nicholas carefully climbed in through the sharp-edged glass.

The raccoon scrambled up onto the firewood and stuck his head through the window. "I think I'll wait out here for you. You just go along inside and look for Oscar," the raccoon said.

Nicholas looked doubtfully at the raccoon.

"It will be all right. Tell him Harold sent you." With those words, the raccoon dropped out of sight.

It was dark and quiet in the shed. The boatbuilders had finished for the day. The building smelled of cedar shavings and fresh paint. Long shadows lay on the floor. A haze of fine sawdust still hung in the air.

"Oscar," Nicholas whispered. Nicholas heard something up in the rafters. He hesitated on the floor. He didn't want to go back out the window and face the raccoon again. He stood in the middle of the room, afraid to make a move.

Three gray squirrels came out of the shadows from around the big brick, central chimney. They chattered away to themselves. They surrounded Nicholas. "What are you doing in this shed?" one of the squirrels asked.

"I am looking for Oscar," he said. "I was told I could

find him in this boat-building shed. Harold said I could ask for his help."

The three squirrels raced away, tumbling over each other and chattering to each other. They came back after circling the shed.

"You know Harold?" the first squirrel asked. "Come with us."

The squirrels took off into the shadows again. Nicholas didn't know where they were taking him, but he wanted to see Oscar and perhaps learn where Francis had gone. He followed the squirrels into the dark building.

Chapter
Twenty Three

Nicholas followed the quick-moving squirrels. He scrambled under the ribs of a small boat, upside down awaiting its planking. He sneezed as he made his way through a pile of sawdust. The squirrels bounded up a narrow set of stairs to a loft. "Come," the squirrels beckoned. "We will take you to the cricket."

"Cricket?" Nicholas said to the fleeing squirrels. "I thought we were going to see a squirrel."

The squirrels beckoned him forward. They were out over the main part of the building. Nicholas looked down at the workspace below. It made him dizzy as he walked along the timbers supporting the roof.

The squirrels brought him into the space where the chimney pierced the roof. Two boards set between the chimney and the roof formed a small space called a cricket. It was dim and hot inside the space.

"Welcome to the cricket," a croaking old voice said. "I heard you have been looking for me."

Nicholas jumped at the voice. As Nicholas got used to the dim light he saw an old gray squirrel, his big tail curled around his body. His red eyes focused on Nicholas.

"Why is this place called a cricket?" Nicholas asked. "Are you Oscar? Harold said you might be able to help me."

"You are full of questions, little mouse. Tell me, what is your name?"

"I am Nicholas. I have been traveling for a long time. I am searching for my Cousin Francis. He had learned some history of our family, and he came south to this area."

"Ah, there is much history to learn in this area," Oscar said. "The history is tied to the Kennebec River." The old squirrel gestured toward the unseen water flowing by the museum. "This region relied on the river for food, transportation, and business."

"Can you tell me the history?" Nicholas asked the old squirrel. "It might help me figure out where I can find my cousin."

"You will learn much more if you experience history. I will send you down the river with a friend. A merganser I know, Etta, will tell you about the river and its history as you travel. It will stay with you, don't you think?" The old gray squirrel coughed.

"I need my rest now, Nicholas. Etta often fishes in the shallows along the bank. Good-bye, Nicholas. I hope you find what you are looking for." The old gray squirrel fell asleep.

Nicholas found Harold snooping around the garbage barrels outside the boat-building barn.

"It's never too early for lunch, wouldn't you say?" Harold said. He had half a boiled egg in his paws. "Did you find Oscar? How is the old squirrel? Tell me all about it on our way to the river. This boiled egg needs a little washing."

Nicholas described his meeting with Oscar. Harold sat on the shore among the reeds. The museum boats bobbed in the quiet current. He munched on the boiled egg. Nicholas was hungry, too. A half-eaten apple bobbed in the water. It was just out of reach. Nicholas stretched his front paws and gripped the ground with his back paws. He could just touch the apple. It spun in the water. Nicholas lost his grip on the ground and splashed into the water.

He came up sputtering and shivering. He felt a boost from underneath, and he flew out of the water, landing with a wet flop on the grass. He shook out his fur. A red-and-white duck with a green head floated in the water, laughing.

"That was quite a trick, little mouse," the merganser said. "If you're not careful, you'll end up as lunch for a snapping turtle."

"I was trying to get that apple." He pointed at the fruit that still bobbed nearby.

"Let me help you," the merganser said. She nudged the apple toward the shore.

Nicholas grabbed it with his paws. He dragged it up on to the bank and took a bite. "Thank you," Nicholas said after a few bites of food. "I feel much better now. Are you Etta? Oscar told me I would find you in the

river. He says you know all about this river and the history of this area."

"Well, I do know some things," Etta said. "I've lived here all my life. I heard many stories growing up on the river."

"Oscar told me I should hear some of those stories. He says we should learn history by experiencing it. If I know about the past, it might help me find my Cousin Francis," Nicholas said.

"I can show you the river," Etta said. "But you have to promise to try and not fall in again. This river is deep and the water moves quickly."

"I'll be careful," Nicholas said. "When can we go?"

"Let's wait for the tide to turn. It will be much easier to float down the river with the tide instead of trying to fight the incoming current."

Harold wandered up, licking his paws after finishing his lunch. "Ah, there you are, Nicholas. I see you have found Etta."

"Hello Harold, I don't often see you around during the day," Etta said.

"Yes, well, I was just headed home for a nap. Etta, you can watch out for this little mouse. I have my own worries." Harold waddled up the slope to spend the heat of the day under one of the museum buildings.

"Come along, Nicholas, the tide is turning." Nicholas hopped on Etta's back. She swam out into the wide, smooth-flowing water. Nicholas hoped the river would lead him to his cousin.

Chapter Twenty Four

Etta and Nicholas set off downstream. Nicholas looked around. They floated away from the city of Bath and the big Route One bridge. The noise of steel shipbuilding from Bath Iron Works echoed under the bridge.

"You know, Nicholas, so much history has happened on the Kennebec," Etta said. "The first European settlement in New England, trading, lumbering, ice harvesting, shipbuilding, and fishing—these have all taken place on this river."

Nicholas looked at the water slowly flowing toward the ocean. He could not see far into the dark water. He imagined all the people through history who must have traveled up and down this river, just as he was now. He remembered his father telling him about his own family.

"My family came with the first settlers to New England. We are all from Massachusetts," Nicholas told Etta.

"The first Europeans to settle in New England came to the mouth of this river. The natives called the river Sagadahoc," Etta said. "The settlers were here before the Pilgrims in Plimoth Colony, and the same year settlers landed at Jamestown in Virginia."

"How come I've never heard of them?" Nicholas asked. "My family knows all the stories of long ago. What happened to them? Do their families still live in Maine?"

"They started a colony, just like at Plymouth, but they didn't stay. Maine in the winter can be a very cold place. After one winter, they built a ship and sailed away," Etta said.

"It must have been scary," Nicholas said to Etta.

"What must have been scary?" Etta asked.

"To be alone in this wild place, with no help and your family thousands of miles away," Nicholas said. "And, after all that work, to leave everything you had built."

"But they made a start. In time, others came and stayed," Etta said. "Now we are here, part of the history of the state. We play a role in history; even if it is just to live in a place that others found long ago."

The two floated along, thinking about the flow of history and their place in it. A bald eagle flapped his wings going up river.

"Hello," Nicholas called out to the passing bird. "I met an eagle who took me all the way to Moosehead Lake."

"Nicholas, that eagle will do more than scare you if he hasn't eaten today. You've been to Moosehead Lake?" Etta asked. "That's where this river starts. It flows past many cities and towns. The state capital, Augusta, is built on the river."

"Did you know, Nicholas, that settlers from the Plimoth Colony came up this river? They had a trading post where Augusta is today. They traveled by sea up the coast to trade with the natives," Etta said.

"I traveled to Maine on a boat," Nicholas told Etta. "It was a wooden schooner, built right here in this state."

"Thousands of ships were built and launched on this river," Etta said. She and Nicholas floated along the Arrowsic Island. The forest, mixed with sheer granite ledge, came right down to the water's edge.

"Bath Iron Works is the last shipyard on the Kennebec," Etta said. "Once, over a hundred years ago, when wooden ships were being built, there were as many as twenty shipyards in the city of Bath itself." The two floated along looking at the forested land.

"The trees on this island and all the surrounding land were cut down to build ships," Etta continued.

"Bath-built ships sailed all the seas," Etta said. "The water of the Kennebec River has traveled all over the world," Etta said, splashing it with her beak.

"Long ago, in the winter, men cut huge blocks of ice out of the river. It was packed in sawdust and shipped to far-off ports."

Nicholas tried to imagine a ship full of ice sailing off to distant lands. He thought about what it would be like to sail on a big ship out on the deep ocean. He leaned over on Etta's back, pretending he was standing on the deck of a sailing ship heeling in the wind.

They had reached the mouth of the river. Ocean waves washed into the river. Seguin Island, with its big lighthouse on top of the hill, was ahead.

"Hey, what are you doing back there?" Etta called. "You're making it hard for me to steer around the lobster buoys."

Etta and Nicholas floated through a patch of color-fully painted buoys. Nearby, a lobster boat was going from buoy to buoy. Nicholas teetered one way then another on Etta's back. Finally, he lost his balance and tumbled into the water. Etta spun around when she heard the splash. Nicholas came up swimming. The lobster boat came between Nicholas and the merganser.

Nicholas swam as fast as he could for the nearest lobster buoy. He clung to the red-and-white float. The captain reached down with her gaff, hooked the buoy, and reeled it aboard. Nicholas clung to the rope and landed on the deck. Etta squawked, but the loud boat engine muffled her voice.

The lobster boat hauled the trap connected to the other end of the buoy. Etta swam around the lobster boat, but did not see Nicholas. As she was still looking, the boat's motor revved up. Etta watched as the boat headed south. It was quiet again, except for the surf pounding ashore at Popham Beach. Nicholas was gone.

Chapter Twenty Five

The lobster boat rocked in the waves. Nicholas slid from side to side as seawater sloshed back and forth over the painted deck. A small, half-round hole in the side of the boat let water run back out to the ocean. He could see Etta through it. She was swimming around the buoys, watching the boat motor away.

Nicholas looked out from under the side deck. There were two people on the boat. One, dressed in orange rubber pants and green boots, steered the boat. A girl, wearing the same orange pants and long orange gloves, stacked empty traps against the stern. Looking down, she noticed Nicholas on the deck.

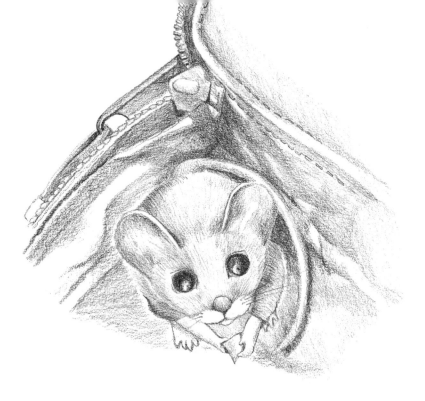

"Well, look at that! I don't believe I've ever seen a mouse out here before," the girl said. She squatted down, smiling at Nicholas. "Hello there, little fella. You sure must be lost." She scooped up Nicholas in her gloved hands. "You're soaked right down to your skin," the girl said. She wrapped Nicholas in a towel hanging inside the cabin.

"You'll never believe it, Mom," the girl said to the woman driving the boat. "Look what I found." She held Nicholas wrapped in the towel close to her mother's face.

The mother, concentrating on steering, looked over. "My goodness, Becca. Where on earth did he come from? Did you fish him up in one of our traps?"

"I found him right on the deck. He's about as cute as a spotted pig, isn't he?" Becca had dried Nicholas off. He finally stopped shivering. He wiggled around in Becca's hands, sniffing the rubber gloves.

"Why, he looks hungry," Becca said. "I think I'll take him below and find him something to eat."

It was noisy below near the growling diesel engine. Heat from the motor warmed the cabin. Becca opened her lunch pail, emptied its contents, and set Nicholas inside along with the towel. She gave him a few saltines.

"You sit right there, little fella. I'll be back just as soon as I finish cleaning up on deck. We're headed for Portland to sell our catch," Becca said.

Nicholas held a cracker in his paws and nibbled at one edge. The boat was moving quickly over the waves with a regular rise and fall. Nicholas, warm at last and full from his lunch, let the motion of the boat rock him to sleep.

He dreamed he was back on the Gloucester fishing boat. He and his friend Edward had found themselves on the seagoing boat. They had helped save it from sinking. He heard shouts and noise come to him through his sleep. He woke, not to a sinking fishing boat, but to the lobster boat, tied to a pier. He looked up through the cabin door and saw Becca and her mom unloading their catch.

A hoist on the pier lifted the totes of lobsters from the boat. Becca's mom discussed the price of lobster with the buyer on the pier. Nicholas made his way to the deck.

"Aren't you a clever little mouse," Becca said. "How'd you get out of that lunch pail?"

Nicholas let her pick him up.

"I've been thinking," Becca said. "It would be fun to have a pet with me when we go out to haul traps. I could make you a little box up by the wheel where you could watch everything. What do you think?" She stroked Nicholas on his back.

Nicholas thought about his cousin and the journal. He thought if Edward was with him, they would find Francis and he could go home.

"But," Becca continued, "it probably wouldn't be much fun for you, would it? So, my mom thought I should set you free where you will be safe. I know just the place."

Nicholas wiggled his whiskers. He liked this smart young girl.

"Come on, Mom will be busy with the lobster buyer for a while. I'll take you ashore now." Becca changed out of her rubber overalls and brought along her lunch pail for Nicholas.

They crossed Commercial Street and headed to the old port. There were shops and restaurants, tourists and business people. Becca dodged the traffic and walked along the sidewalk up Exchange Street. She bought a strawberry ice-cream cone for herself and another empty cone for Nicholas. She sat on a bench in

Monument Square and ate the ice cream. Nicholas sat in the open lunch pail in Becca's lap and crunched on his empty sugar cone.

When they had finished eating, Becca walked along busy Congress Street, then over the hill. They came at last to Deering Oaks, a big park with a baseball field, paths for walking, and a big pond. Becca let Nicholas down in the grass.

It felt good to Nicholas to set his paws on solid ground.

Becca squatted down next to him. "I bet you'll find a nice home here," she said.

Nicholas looked up at the kind girl.

"You go on now," Becca said.

Nicholas squeaked his thanks and scurried off. Becca stood on the edge of the park under a spreading oak tree. On a nearby path, a dog barked. A chipmunk sitting on a branch of the tree, holding an acorn in his hands, chattered away excitedly.

"Oh, you hush now, Mr. Chipmunk," Becca said. "What are you going on about?" She headed back to the boat and her mom. The chipmunk ran down the tree and off into the park.

Chapter Twenty Six

Nicholas wandered into the park. The canopy of old hardwood trees stretched across the mown lawn. It was getting near fall. Some of the maple leaves had already started to turn colors. Nicholas liked the feeling of the short grass under his paws and the rustling leaves over his head.

A boy and girl walked a young dog on the tar path. The dog, a mix of breeds, strained at his leash. "Heel, Parker," the boy called out. The boy pulled back on the leash, trying to keep the dog at their side. The dog, sniffing along the ground, had picked up the scent of something.

Parker whined, tugging on the leash. Nicholas sensed the dog was after him and took off under the trees. Parker could not control himself any longer. He gave one big tug and chased after little Nicholas.

In the tree near the road, a chipmunk sitting on a branch nibbled on an acorn. He looked to see what the dog was after. He saw a small brown mouse take off around the tree. The mouse looked familiar. The chipmunk chattered excitedly, and ran off after the dog and the mouse.

Nicholas tried to keep ahead of the dog. The dog dragged his leash on the ground as he ran. The boy and girl ran through the park, calling for their dog. Nicholas ducked under a weeping willow near a pond. The dog followed him, brushing into the low-hanging branches. The dog disappeared from sight. The boy and girl ran by the tree. The chipmunk ran after them all, huffing and puffing as he tried to keep up.

Inside the willow branches, Nicholas ran around the tree trunk. The dog sniffed, and barked, and chased the mouse. The leash wrapped around a branch, stopping the dog cold. The dog yelped and sat down. Nicholas popped out from under the willow branches

and found himself at the edge of a pond. A fountain in the middle of the pond sprayed water into the air.

The dog continued to bark and tug at his leash inside the tree branches. The boy and girl heard their dog and headed back toward the willow tree. The girl ducked under the branches. "There you are, Parker. Why did you run away?" The dog was panting and slobbering in his excitement. He got up and strained on the leash stuck on the branch.

The chipmunk, a bit winded, finally caught up to the group. He avoided all the excitement and went around the willow tree. He spotted the mouse standing on the shore of the pond looking at a small island not far away. A perfect-sized house for a mouse sat in the middle of the little island. A family of mallards sat on the front lawn. The house was a cheery bright red with white trim. It reminded Nicholas of farmers' houses out in western Massachusetts, his home.

There was a loud crack from under the tree. The branch on which the dog's leash had tangled broke and flew out and splashed in the pond near Nicholas. The girl lunged at the dog's leash and caught him, just as he was about to take off. "Come on you, I've had enough walking in the park for one day." She tugged on the dog's leash, dragging him home.

Near the pond, Nicholas looked at the branch floating in the water next to him. Suddenly he heard, "Nicholas, is that you? Nicholas?"

Nicholas stood up and turned around just in time to see a chipmunk barreling at him as fast as his four little legs could travel. "Nicholas! It is you! I've been searching for you for months and months."

Just as he said this, the chipmunk ran into Nicholas and wrapped his front legs around him. He hugged the confused little mouse, and both animals toppled into the water. There was a splash almost as big as the fountain. The two animals came up in the shallow water.

Nicholas wiped the water dripping from his eyes and looked at the chipmunk. "Edward?" Nicholas said quietly. "Edward, is that you?" Nicholas smiled.

"Of course it is me," Edward said. He smiled back and laughed.

Nicholas hugged his friend and they both hopped up and down in the water. They splashed and laughed looking at each other.

"Edward, I can't believe you are here in Portland, Maine, with me. How did you ever find me?"

"Nicholas, I have been looking for you since you left Martha's Vineyard last summer," Edward said. "Of course, I have some wonderful stories to tell you about. I have had my share of adventures, too. I had to do a bit of rescuing other mice, and a poor little red squirrel was quite lost without my help," Edward started.

"I have been traveling for so long, I am amazed that you found me at all," Nicholas said. He stood still in the water. He was dripping wet, but he hardly noticed.

"I have so much to tell you as well." He shivered. The sun was setting earlier now and it would soon be dark.

"We should find some place out of the weather. It would be warm in that house, I'm sure," Edward said.

"Let's use this branch," Nicholas said. The two friends hopped on the branch and paddled their way out to the little house. The animals had been through so much. They crawled inside and covered themselves with duck down. At least my friend is here, each thought of the other. They fell sound asleep.

Chapter Twenty Seven

The next day, Nicholas awoke to the sound of ducks quacking. The family of mallards swam in the shallow water, dipping down for the tender grass growing on the bottom of the pond. The young birds splashed and laughed as they ate. They were getting ready to fly south for the first time.

Edward had been snoring quietly. Even the excitement of the young ducks had not disturbed him. He rolled over when he heard Nicholas speaking. "Nicholas," Edward said, jumping up and rubbing his eyes. "I dreamed I was still searching for you. But here you are, just as I knew I would find you."

"Yes, here I am, Edward, still traveling. I'm still searching for my cousin and our family journal. I'm beginning to think I'll never find it."

"That's just it, Nicholas. I have news for you. I was on my way home when I left you in Plymouth. I had a wonderful Thanksgiving at home. We had all the trimmings, cranberries, pinecones, and the tenderest mushrooms. Everyone in my family was so surprised I made it home. They really embarrassed me with their concern."

"Edward, please tell me what news you have for me," Nicholas said, tugging on Edward's paw.

"Well, you see, after we ate, we were sitting around digesting. My great-aunt and uncle had come down from the White Mountains. They told the strangest story."

"Edward, please, what is your news?"

"Now, Nicholas, I'm getting to that," Edward said, clearing his throat. "My great-uncle told us how this mouse had just passed through the National Forest. He was carrying a big family journal."

"Was it my cousin Francis?"

"My uncle said this mouse had come from Maine and was being chased by another animal. This mouse, my uncle didn't know his name, was trying to get as far away from his home as he could. He was trying to hide the journal to keep it safe. And this is when I thought of you, Nicholas. The journal goes right back to the beginnings of the mouse's family, with stories about when mice first came to the New World."

"That must be my cousin," Nicholas shouted. "He's not in Maine at all. Who is chasing him?"

"My uncle didn't know. The mouse only stopped long enough to leave clues in New Hampshire as to where he was going. When I heard the story, I knew I had to find you and tell you."

"Oh, thank you, Edward. I have to get to New Hampshire as quickly as I can. Where are the White Mountains, anyway?"

"I should think they are not hard to find. Why, Nicholas, I would imagine in a very short time you will meet your cousin."

"Do you really think so, Edward? Can you come with me? I don't want to travel alone anymore."

"Nicholas, my friend, of course I will accompany you. We can visit my dear old aunt and uncle. I will have to help you with the clues, you know."

The ducks outside the house were still splashing through their breakfast "Maybe those ducks will help," Nicholas said. "I bet they can take us to New Hampshire." He ran outside and spoke to the mother duck. He told her his story. The mother duck listened, keeping an eye on her young ones. "We are meeting a flock of ducks at Sebago, and then we are all headed south to the Chesapeake."

Nicholas looked crestfallen. "I don't even think we

can get off this little island without some help from someone," he said.

The mother duck sighed again and said, "I'll tell you what. We can give you a lift as far west as Sebago. From there it's a short way to New Hampshire."

"That would be wonderful," Nicholas said. "Edward, did you hear that?"

Nicholas and Edward waited while the mother duck finally got her young ones sorted out. Nicholas rode with the mother and Edward sat on the father's back. They set off with a great deal of quacking and splashing. The flight was short. Nicholas looked ahead as the western mountains grew bigger. Edward clung to the father mallard's throat and kept his eyes tightly shut.

They splashed down in Jordan Bay, a section of Sebago Lake, in western Maine. Busy Route 302 passed close to the beach. "Before long, an animal trailer will stop for some water. They will be on their way to the big fair in Fryeburg. You can catch a ride all the way to the border of New Hampshire."

The ducks flew off in search of the great raft of birds gathering for their fall migration. Before long, a horse trailer rolled into the parking lot next to the beach. The driver got out, opened the back, and headed to the lake with a pail. Nicholas and Edward ran up the ramp and between the legs of a grey Persheron horse.

"Who's that?" the horse said, shaking his mane. He scuffed his hooves on the floor of the trailer.

"We need a ride to Fryeburg. Can we go with you?"

Nicholas asked. He had scrambled up to the swinging basket of hay set there for the horse. Before the horse could answer, the driver came back. He hung the bucket on a hook near the horse and slammed the ramp closed.

Edward and Nicholas were off again.

Nicholas looked out through the hay at the passing road. He wondered how he would tell when they were in New Hampshire. Were the trees different? Were the people different? He wondered about the clues Edward had mentioned.

What kinds of clues did his cousin leave and where would they find them? Did Edward's aunt and uncle know any more about Francis? Nicholas looked over at his friend Edward. He was sitting with the Persheron, telling the horse a story about fighting off weasels with one hand while holding a scared red squirrel with the other.

Nicholas laughed to himself. At least his friend would be with him as he traveled through New Hampshire in search of his family and the long lost journal.

mitten press

Mitten Press is proud to launch this series of chapter books about a lively field mouse from Massachusetts. He lives tucked under a farmhouse outside Stockbridge until a flood destroys the journal that contains his family history. In Book One, Nicholas embarks on a journey across Massachusets to locate his long-lost uncle and a copy of the precious journal. Book Two sees Nicholas depart for Maine after finding out that his cousin has taken the journal copy there. As Nicholas will discover, Maine is a very large and diverse state.

The series will chronicle Nicholas's adventures throughout New England. In each book, young readers will learn about another state—the animals that live there, the geography, and even the state's history—as Nicholas continues his search for his family journal.

Coming soon ...

Nicholas: A New Hampshire Tale
ISBN: 978-1-58726-521-1

Join Nicholas's New England readers by sending your e-mail address to the publisher at ljohnson@mittenpress.com. You will receive updates as new books in the series are completed and fun activities to challenge what you know about the New England states.